OPEN FOR WITCHNESS

HAUNTED HAVEN MYSTERIES
BOOK THREE

ADA BELL

EMPRESS BOOKS

PRAISE FOR ADA BELL

"*Mystic Pieces* is a charming, humorous, and original mystery that weaves a tale of murder and self-discovery with heart, family, and psychic visions."

— READERS' FAVORITE

"...I liked Aly as a main character and reading about her and her powers. I liked the side characters and how each had their own personality that made it easy to remember. All in all I really enjoyed this book and look forward to the next book in the series!"

— LOLA'S BOOK REVIEWS

"A cute and cozy introduction to the quirky and devoted characters, *Mystic Pieces* is the perfect first installment to the Shady Grove Psychic Mystery Series."

— LITERARY LIONESS

OPEN FOR WITCHNESS

Enjoy this charming third installment of the Haunted Haven series by award-winning author Ada Bell.

With two solved murders under her belt, Emma agrees to tackle a mystery that's been haunting the residents of neighboring Shady Grove for years: what supernatural presence keeps the only bar in town from operating? Emma's been in haunted places before, and no one else ever noticed. The ghosts she's encountered may not have all been warm and fuzzy, bu they were peaceful. Intrigued, she and her friend Ben head to the bar he hopes to take over. The last thing she expects is to find a ghostly sentry at the door, preventing anyone from going in. Since ghosts don't wear clothes, Emma's thread magic is of little use. Still, she made a promise, so she'll do her best to find out who died and how to bring them peace.

Her inquiries reveal a murder in the bar twenty years ago. The only way to help Ben fulfill his dream of owning his own bar is to solve the mystery—but the trail has been cold for decades. Can she close the case to help Ben reopen the bar before the spirits close her down for good?

Open for Witchness is a paranormal cozy mystery set in a small town, with ghosts, witches, and a talking cat. Oh my! Fans of Angie Fox, Amy Boyles, and Annabel Chase will love this bewitching series.

ALSO BY ADA BELL

Shady Grove Psychic Mysteries

Mystic Pieces

The Scry's the Limit

Sight Seering

Mystic Treasure (Book 3.5)

Seer Today, Gone Tomorrow

The Pie in the Scry

Mystic Persons

The Psychic's the Thing

Haunted Haven Series

Unfinished Witchness

Risky Witchness

Open for Witchness

Bundles and Boxed Sets

Shady Grove Psychic Mysteries 1-3

Shady Grove Psychic Mysteries 4-6

Haunted Haven Mysteries 1-3

Empress Books

P.O. Box 1572

Clifton Park, NY 12019

Haunted Haven

For everyone who believes in magic.

And all the talking cats out there.

"I ain't afraid of no ghosts." - Ray Parker, Jr., *Ghostbusters*

On television, professional ghost hunters carried recorders, electronic equipment, headphones, and other fancy gadgets. Those people needed to convince a skeptical television audience of their legitimacy.

As a witch seeking to fit into small town life, my goal was to look inconspicuous while searching for supernatural activity. Instead of recording evidence and leaving, I needed to find a ghost and assist with any unresolved business troubling them since roughly the turn of the century.

A tall order for a mere mortal.

Okay, also a tall order for me, forty-two-year-old Emma Faden. For most of my life, I'd been a regular person. A pretty boring one, actually. Dull strawberry-blond hair, dull skin, depressing job history, lackluster life. Then I'd inherited my grandfather's magic.

Suddenly, my vibrant red hair shone in silky waves, my complexion glowed, spells flowed from my fingertips, and I saw ghosts. This made me both an excellent person to take on exorcising the local bar and a terrible one.

"You do know what the phrase 'lie low' means, right? Dottie was very specific that you shouldn't call attention to your abilities." This question came from my cat, Pink, as he watched me braid my hair. "Nothing flashy, she said."

I glanced down at myself, pretending to misunderstand. "Black yoga pants, blue sweatshirt, no glitter. What's flashy about this?"

"It's not the outfit and you know it. You're not supposed to use your powers where humans can see!" My extraordinarily old cat took his role as mentor seriously, which is why he'd spent the past several days trying to talk me out of accompanying Ben Cartwright today.

Turning away from the mirror, I met Pink's gaze. Big green eyes full of reproach bored into my hazel ones. "As far as anyone is concerned, I'm walking through an old, run-down bar to see what work it needs to reopen. Things have been rough for Ben since his stepfather died. Running his own bar is his dream, and I am uniquely positioned to help."

"The only thing that place needs is someone to exorcise the ghost, as you well know. If you do it, the whole town will hear about you in a matter of minutes. It's the opposite of lying low."

"Ghost hunters live everywhere. When I was in college, I watched like four different series on TLC. They gave lectures, and I'm pretty sure some do podcasts. I don't want Ben to get scammed."

In my experience, ghosts didn't haunt buildings in the traditional sense. They didn't rattle chains, moan loudly, or cause the room temperature to drop. That's what made it tricky when Ben asked me to remove a ghost from the bar in nearby Shady Grove. Everyone was familiar with the rumors: the bar had been cursed, haunted, or both (although no one knew who did the cursing/haunting or why). Over the past twenty years, the property changed ownership several times, and no one had opened it for business. Finally, the townspeople concluded that a dead teetotal moved in and refused to allow liquor sales in the area.

That this was the most logical and widely accepted explanation told you a lot about Shady Grove, New York.

Since I'd moved to Willow Falls, the rumors surrounding me were almost as plentiful and absurd as those about the bar. The locals noticed my "bed-and-breakfast" entertained few guests. The handful of people who checked in, like Ben, stayed a long time. On top of that, the town gossips said I talked to people who weren't there. After checking in a few weeks ago, Ben witnessed this firsthand. He also probably noticed I didn't charge his credit card: my magic came with an obligation to help others, and my grandfather left me more money than I could ever spend.

When Ben discovered the abandoned bar stood available to anyone who paid the long-overdue tax lien, he asked me to help. Despite knowing nothing about bartending, I agreed immediately.

While Willow Falls was by no means large or densely populated, our small town dwarfed Shady Grove. "Town" was barely accurate. It was like a hamlet where a surprisingly large percentage of the population possessed supernatural abilities.

"What's so special about this bar, anyway?" Pink asked. "Why can't he serve drinks somewhere else?"

"Three reasons," I said, ticking them off on my fingers. "One, there is no open storefront in Shady Grove suitable for a bar that requires less time and money than this one.

Real estate isn't cheap, but this is a tax foreclosure, which makes it affordable. Second, the location makes it an ideal spot for tourists. Third—and most importantly—he lived with his mother in Shady Grove before she remarried and moved them to Willow Falls. He feels closest to her there."

"It's weird hearing you tell my life story to a cat," Ben said.

I grinned. "Just wait."

Ben squatted and scratched Pink's head. "Listen, I know you're worried. I promise I won't let anything hurt Emma."

My cat could be stubborn, but so was I. He knew when he'd lost an argument. He dipped his head before he asked, "Is there anything I can say to change your mind?"

I shook my head, knowing the conversation was already over. "If I get in trouble, I will swear up and down to the Magical Enforcement Office that you tried to stop me. Besides, Walter's coming with us. What could go wrong?"

"What, indeed?" My cat rolled his eyes. "You're hunting spirits with an eighty-year-old man trapped in the body of a twenty-six-year-old ghost who exhibits a four-year-old's utter glee at the world."

"Just because you're cranky, don't take it out on me," my grandfather said, appearing behind the cat. He wore a long-sleeved gray button-up shirt, brown pants, and a black leather jacket with a matching hat. In one hand, he carried an Indiana-Jones-style whip. "We're going on an adventure!"

Pink gave me a "see what I mean?" look. I responded by picking him up and kissing the top of his head. He pretended to hate it, but he tilted his head enough to give me access to scratch the spot under his skin. A small purr escaped.

"This should be quick," I said. "It's purely a recon mission."

In response, my cat sneezed at me. I wasn't sure what to make of that, but he jumped down. When he lifted his rear leg and began taking a bath, I understood him perfectly.

"We love you, too, you stinker," Walter said as he floated over Pink's outstretched toes and out the door. "Come on, slowpoke! Last one to the car is a moldy doughnut!"

A what?

"I wish you could see your face right now," Ben said. "What I wouldn't give to hear this conversation."

"Trust me, you're better off not knowing."

"After you, then." He gave an exaggerated bow and pointed toward the front door. "I realize this was a strange request. Thank you for not changing your mind."

Shaking my head, I stepped over Pink carefully and followed Walter onto the front porch.

Together, we headed for my new Porsche Cayenne Turbo SUV. The car was ridiculously extravagant, but living in the woods in the northeastern US, I needed something more reliable than the twenty-year-old Toyota I'd driven previously. As the ghost who talked me into the purchase pointed out, considering how long I kept my vehicles, I might as well get the best one.

The SUV purred to life beneath my fingertips, making me smile. Absurd price tag or not, I loved my all-leather baby. Ben hopped into the front passenger seat while Walter begrudgingly climbed into the back. He wanted me to make Ben sit there so he could ride shotgun, but, honestly, people found me weird enough already.

After typing the address in my GPS, we were on our way. About twenty miles of wilderness separated Shady

Grove from Willow Falls, with only a single gas station and Dunkin' Donuts to break up the view. It made for a gorgeous drive. With the late fall sun warm on my face and a canopy of trees leading the way, time passed quickly.

The bar sat on Second Street, close enough to the heart of town to still have the raised wooden sidewalks and cobblestone streets found on Main Street. Also close enough that, while not technically bound by Main Street's naming regulations, most businesses followed them.

"Two Mules?" I read from the sign aloud. "Is that a pun?"

"Don't you know your Clint Eastwood references?" Walter asked.

"I can honestly say I do not. Why?"

"Leo was a big fan. That's why the bar is Western-themed. Plus, his last name was West."

Leo owned the bar when it last operated. This information explained a lot about an Old West-style saloon sitting in Upstate New York. After I repeated my grandfather's explanation for Ben's benefit, I returned to my original question.

"Clint Eastwood played a mule in a movie?"

"He made a film called *Two Mules for Sister Sara*. A mule is also a type of alcoholic beverage. It's pun-adjacent." Walter shook his head. "You're hopeless."

A random thought flew through my head: what if the place was haunted by someone who hated not alcohol but puns? Maybe if we called it "Ben's Bar," the ghost would take off, and he could open for business this afternoon.

Shaking the ridiculous notion aside, I pulled into a parking spot across the street and studied the building's exterior. From my perspective, the bar looked like any abandoned building. Weathered boards covered the windows. The once-vibrant sign hung at an angle. It looked like the building had old-time swinging saloon doors, but on closer inspection, they'd been painted onto an actual door. Since Shady Grove was roughly three thousand miles from the Old West and received significant snowfall each year, I appreciated the practicality. Boarded-up windows suggested an apartment above the bar, which was common in the area.

No sign of anything supernatural.

The oddest part was the yellow caution tape around the sidewalk, including between the adjacent buildings. Big barrels blocked the walkway on either side. But why? Unless there was something wrong with the wooden planks, people should be allowed to use the path.

Was the ghost scaring away customers from the neighboring businesses, too? The bar sat nestled between two other storefronts, and maybe those owners didn't want their customers to get spooked. On the left, a delightful-looking building with pink and white awnings displayed rows of chocolate goodies in the windows. Candy canes held up the wooden sign offering the store's name.

"Remind me to drop by Cocoa Channel on the way out," I said, nodding toward it.

"You don't want to check out Bait and Switch?" Ben pointed to an enormous wooden fish sign to the right of the bar.

"To meet the owner? Sure, after we inspect the bar. To buy tackle? No, thanks."

"Maybe one of those businesses put up the yellow tape."

"I guess. Is flimsy plastic supposed to keep a ghost inside the bar?"

The idea of a spirit causing trouble for their neighbors

intrigued me. Over the past several months, I'd encountered three separate ghosts, including my grandfather. None of them could speak with any living person other than me. The only way they could manipulate the human world was by asking me to do things. Walter perfected that one not long after we met. But if he rattled chains, only I'd be aware of it.

What made this bar different? Was it haunted, or did someone push that theory to keep Shady Grove a bar-free zone? We still had some dry towns in the neighboring counties. Someone might want Shady Grove to be one of them.

"Stop stalling!" Walter yelled in my ear, making me jump. "I want to meet this ghost!"

Although his methods weren't appreciated, my grandfather was right. I'd been staring at the bar long enough; it was time to go inside.

I turned toward Ben. "Are you ready?"

"Ready to confront a possibly evil, definitely not-alive person?" He grinned at me nervously. "Of course I am! Why wouldn't I be?"

"We can leave. This is your gig."

"No, I want to go in. Sitting here, I feel dumb asking you to come. It's just a building needing a lot of work, surrounded by an urban legend. I can go in myself."

"I'm happy to be here. It's not every day your friend buys a famous building."

"Don't get excited yet," Ben said. "It's not mine. The town clerk said I could check the inside before deciding whether to buy the tax lien."

"They let you do that?"

"Not usually, no. But Manuel is a friend of a friend." Ben held up a key. "Don't tell anyone I have this."

"Your secret is safe with me."

He took a deep breath, as if bracing himself. "Let's go. The sooner we get inside, the sooner I own a bar."

Over my shoulder, I spoke to Walter. "You awake back there?"

Nothing.

When he didn't reply, I unbuckled and turned fully around. The back seat was empty. I craned my neck but couldn't see anything other than a basketball left by T, the teenager living at Haven.

"Where did he go? He didn't pop back to the mansion, did he?" The question was mostly to myself, since Ben couldn't see or hear my grandfather. I'd hesitated about even explaining that he'd be coming along, but Ben's mother told him about my ghostly connections after her late husband and I convinced her to confess to murder.

"What's wrong?"

Before I could answer, a massive, ghostly head appeared two inches from my nose. I screamed.

Walter cackled. While I'd been examining the bar, he'd exited the back of the SUV and come around to surprise me. Now, while his body remained on the street, he'd stuck his head through the closed window. "Come on! What are you waiting for?"

"I was looking for you," I grumbled. "Can you please back up so I don't have to move through you?"

He laughed again. Pink's description of a small child's joie de vivre had been spot-on.

"Everything's fine," I said to Ben. "He's just having fun. Let's go in."

When I opened the car door, a gust of wind blew it shut. Given the stillness in the air on the way here, that surprised me. Our weather changed frequently, but the timing sent a shiver down my spine. Trying to sound confident, I turned to Ben. "Probably a coincidence."

He looked unsure but nodded.

On the second try, I stepped out of the vehicle without incident. After a moment, Ben joined me. About halfway across the street, I stopped and put my hand on his arm.

The building throbbed, glowering at me as if it didn't want me to go inside. In my head, that sounded ridiculous. Buildings weren't sentient. And yet, the rage vibrated in my bones.

"Do you feel that?" I whispered.

"Yeah. I don't know what it is, but it's wrong. I should go in first."

As badly as I wanted to hide behind my thirty-five-year-old, well-muscled friend, he'd asked me here as a professional. I was the witch who spoke to ghosts. His muscles would be useless against the supernatural.

"No, I'm okay," I said. "I want to talk to them."

Before taking another step, I pulled out my phone and swiped to the camera app. Whatever happened, it seemed wise to make a record for later. If nothing else, I wanted to know whether the building's malevolence would come through to others watching the video.

Taking a deep breath, I focused my gaze on the dual windows at the top, as if they were the eyes of the building. I took another step.

A hiss filled my ears. I glanced back at Ben, who looked very uneasy. "Is this normal?"

"I'm here to help," I called. "I'm not going to hurt anyone."

After a moment, I stepped forward again. A sound made me hesitate, but when no one appeared, I kept moving toward the bar. Once I got inside, we could figure out what was happening.

The low hissing continued.

The moment I ducked under the police tape and stepped onto the raised wooden planks of the sidewalk, the hiss intensified into a full-blown growl. A blur shot through the doors.

Was that a cat?

My brain barely had time to finish the thought before the blur slammed into my chest. I stumbled backward. My feet scrambled off the edge of the raised wooden sidewalk. I fell.

Ben called my name.

Walter screamed.

Pain exploded in my skull. Everything went black.

TWO

A soft beeping woke me. My alarm? I raised an arm to turn it off, only to realize something attached me to the bed. My eyes flew open.

The sterile room around me was completely unfamiliar. Now that I thought about it, these rough white sheets weren't mine, nor was the scratchy gown I wore.

Wires connected me to a machine beside the bed, which explained the beeping. A tube in my arm led to an IV stand in the corner, leaving no doubt as to my location.

A hospital.

What happened? How did I get here?

The last thing I knew, I'd been walking to the bar. Something came through the door and attacked me. The various ghosts I'd met frequently moved through solid objects, so that didn't surprise me, but the attack did. The spirit should have passed right through me.

Was I wrong? Maybe I'd been so startled by the ghost's sudden appearance, I'd jumped and fallen off the sidewalk. It seemed plausible, but the throbbing in my ribs suggested otherwise.

At least I'd confirmed the rumors: the bar was quite definitely haunted. Not only did the building have a resident supernatural being, it was unlike anything I'd ever experienced. My attacker wasn't a human ghost. The growling, the hissing, none of it made sense. As bizarre as it sounded, I could've sworn I heard a cat right before getting hit.

Could the ghost have a pet? Was the bar haunted by a house cat? I didn't have the slightest idea how to help a feline resolve unfinished business. What did I do, bring him mice to chase or offer some catnip?

"You're awake!" My friend Josie, who worked at the mansion as the cook, stepped into view. I blinked several times to verify she wasn't a mirage. Josie didn't leave the house much.

"How did you get here? Are we in a room at the mansion I never noticed?"

She squeezed my hand. "We're at Willow Falls Memorial Hospital. The ambulance brought you here after you fainted."

Oh, right. She was my emergency contact.

"I fainted?"

"That's what Ben told the operator when he called 911. If he lied, you let me know and there won't be anything left when the police come to arrest him."

Her fierce loyalty made me chuckle. Then I winced as my head throbbed. Although an IV line limited my mobility, I reached around with my left hand and found a lump behind my ear. "He lied, but Ben didn't do this. Something didn't want us to enter the bar."

"Are you sure?"

"He was standing at least ten feet away when it slammed into me. Unfortunately, I don't know what *it* was.

Walter should be able to tell me; he saw everything." I looked around the room. "Where is Walter?"

"I can't see him," she reminded me gently.

Right. I must've gotten knocked on the head pretty hard to forget.

Back to the immediate question: where had my grandfather gone? If we weren't home, he went where I went. When the ambulance transported me to the hospital, he should have been pulled along. He couldn't control where we went, and he couldn't stray far from me. I wasn't sure exactly how far, but my best estimate was around a hundred yards. The hospital was many miles from the bar.

As long as I wore my magical locket, the one spelled to allow me to travel with Walter, he should be nearby.

Instinctively, my left hand went to my neck.

"It's gone!" I gasped. "Where is it?"

"Your necklace?" Josie nodded as if realization dawned on her at the same moment. "If you were wearing it when the paramedics showed up, it should be with the rest of your belongings. I'm glad you said something. Walter must be beside himself if he saw you get knocked out and then found himself deposited at home without you. Poor guy."

"Would you be willing to go to him? I feel terrible." The spell only worked while I wore the necklace. When it came off, Walter went back to the mansion. Even if someone brought me the locket immediately and I slid it over my head, he'd stay there until I returned home.

"We should get an answering machine," Josie said. "One of the old ones. That way, when we need to convey information to your grandfather, someone can call and leave a message."

I smiled at her. "I'll get one. Do you know when I can leave?"

She shook her head and stood. "No, but I'll tell the doctor you're awake. Also, Ben is waiting in the hall."

"He's here? Why didn't he go home?"

"Oh, he's overreacting. I think he's slightly worried he might have accidentally gotten you killed. No big deal."

I chuckled, but the pain lancing through my side turned it into a wince. "This isn't his fault. Please, send him in."

After a gentle hug, Josie let a sheepish-looking Ben into the room on her way out. He apologized about thirty times without meeting my eyes.

"Hey. Look at me," I said.

He shook his head. "This shouldn't have happened."

"True, but you didn't do this. Something attacked me. You couldn't have known what was going to happen. Can you see ghosts?"

"Not that I know of."

"Did you talk to anyone who sees ghosts, get information you failed to share with me?"

Finally, he met my eyes. "You're the only person I know who sees ghosts."

"Exactly." His loyalty made me smile. "What did you see before I fell?"

"Walking up to the bar, I sensed a negative energy. It swooped in like when a thunderstorm comes up out of nowhere. Something growled. Did you hear that, too?"

"In retrospect, the angry breeze may have been a warning."

"You think? It was the strangest thing. You were walking toward the bar. Something shot through the closed door. You flew backward and landed in the street." He winced. "There wasn't time to catch you. You smacked your head on the cobblestones."

"What hit me?"

He hesitated. "I'm not sure."

"I know this sounds weird, but to me, it looked like a cat."

"Yes! I thought so, too! A big brown and white cat, but transparent."

Unbelievable. Ben couldn't see ghosts, usually, but he'd spotted the same thing I did. Were only human ghosts invisible to other people? A whole new world of possibility unfolded.

"That's exactly what I thought," I said. "But I don't know how or why you could have seen it."

"Why wouldn't I? Lots of people reported weird things in and around the bar over the years. I expected if the ghost was real, we'd both see it."

"You can't see Walter." That reminded me. "What happened to my necklace? Did the paramedics take it? My heart-shaped locket."

"I didn't notice. Sorry."

Panic threatened to overwhelm me. I couldn't lose my necklace. It was priceless. I'd promised Walter to show him the modern world. I could do the incantation linking him to the locket again, but the main reason it worked was because of its ties to our family. The locket contained pictures of Walter and my grandmother, Vera, when they were together. She'd returned the necklace on the day she left him, and their devastation strengthened the spell.

Ben must have seen my face fall because he said, "I'll ask the doctors. But first... this might not be a good time, but I have to tell you something."

"Something more upsetting than losing an irreplaceable heirloom because an enormous dead cat attacked me?"

With a wince, he pulled an object out of his pocket. It was twisted, melted. The whole thing was so mangled it took me a minute to recognize it as my iPhone. "You, uh, dropped this when you fell."

"Did it fall into a barrel of acid?" The phone could be replaced, but the extensive damage sent a chill down my spine. "I don't understand what happened. I was expecting a ghost."

"Apparently, there is a ghost. Just less friendly than we expected. The whole thing scared the wits out of me. For a minute, I thought..." He swallowed hard and blinked.

"It's okay. I'm fine. I just wish I understood." My first inclination was to call my mentor, Dottie, but, well, her number was in my phone.

"What about a poltergeist? Are those real?"

"I've never met one, but that doesn't mean they don't exist. I need to do some research," I said. "Did the doctors tell you anything about my condition?"

"Sorry, no. HIPAA. If I hadn't ridden in with you, I don't think they would have confirmed you were even here."

"You rode in the ambulance?" He nodded. "Please tell me my six-week old Porsche Cayenne doesn't look like my phone. Lie if you must."

For the first time since walking into the room, he smiled. "No, your car is fine. We'll have to go back and get it, but it was outside the attack zone. Not a scratch on it."

Thank goodness.

The wave of relief following his statement came attached to the realization that I felt terrible. My chest throbbed like a battering ram had hit me. There were also tiny pinpricks that I strongly suspected would fit the pattern of a cat's claws when I checked after Ben left.

"I'm glad you're okay, but I should go back," he said.

"To the bar? Stay far away from the bar. You think you're immune to an angry ghost?"

Ben heaved a sigh. "I feel so useless."

"You're not useless. Getting killed would make you useless."

"I might be fine."

"Or the ghost might drop the ceiling on your head. We don't know what it can do," I pointed out.

"Right. I'll wait."

"Thank you. I need to know what we're dealing with before I risk either of us going back. If you want to help, distract me by telling me about your plans for the bar once it's de-haunted."

His face lit up, and he started talking animatedly. Changing the subject was definitely the best way to cheer us up. I was too tired to focus on the words, but his enthusiasm helped me relax.

A few minutes later, the door opened. A Hispanic woman in a white lab coat stuck her head in. When she saw me, a broad smile crossed her face. "Emma! I'm so glad you're awake. I'm Dr. Lopez. How do you feel?"

"Like I got hit by a bus."

"That's my cue," Ben said, standing up. "Do you need me to do anything for you?"

"Can you take T to pick up my car?" The teenager staying at the mansion, whose full name was Terrence, would be thrilled at the opportunity. "Josie can give you my spare keys."

Once he'd gone, Dr. Lopez sat in the chair Ben had vacated. When she spoke, her brown eyes were gentle. "What happened?"

"I fell off the sidewalk," I said with a wince. "They're not raised where I'm from. It's so embarrassing."

"Yes, that's what your friend said. Emma, did he push

you? Hurt you in any way?" Her eyes searched for any sign of deception.

"No! He absolutely did not." I couldn't tell her the truth, but I could emphatically reassure her that Ben had nothing to do with my injuries. "He was standing by the car."

"Why?"

I shrugged. "We went ghost-hunting, because of the rumors about the bar. I'm sure you've heard them. The whole thing was silly. Ben wasn't as excited as me. When we pulled up, I raced for the door. I should have gone slower. Maybe I hit a loose board or something."

She paused. "Do you feel safe at home?"

The question almost made me burst out laughing. Did I, a hearth witch, feel safe in my magical mansion with dozens of protection spells layered into it over the past fifty years? Not to mention the cooking witch in the kitchen, the family ghost, and my magical cat. "Yes, absolutely."

"How long have you known Mr. Cartwright?"

"Almost two months. He's been staying at my bed-and-breakfast since his stepfather died. He sleeps on a different floor. We're not romantically involved." I took a deep breath. "This was an accident, and Ben had nothing to do with it."

After a long moment, she nodded. "I'm inclined to believe you. Although your injuries seem too severe for a minor fall, there's no alternate theory. No signs of being pushed. No bruises consistent with someone grabbing you or pulling you backward."

"You didn't see anything on my front? No bruising or anything?" Her eyes narrowed. Hastily, I added, "I had the weirdest idea that I got hit by a stray paintball."

"That's a better theory than anything I came up with," she said as she rose. "But, no. There's not a scratch on your front. Very bizarre. I've never seen anything like it. The police are coming to take a report. Be sure to mention your paintball theory to them."

"The police?"

"We have to report all suspicious injuries. It's routine."

"There's no need for them to come here," I said. "I can stop by the station on my way home."

"Not today, you can't. We're keeping you under observation for twenty-four hours. We need to do some tests, make sure whatever caused your fall wasn't a medical issue."

My heart sank at her words. A whole day? I had to stay here, away from everything?

"No, that's not right. I have to get home."

"What's more important than figuring out why you fell?"

Since I knew what happened, checking on Walter seemed much more important. He'd been closer to the bar than Ben; what did he see?

But I couldn't tell her that, so I leaned back against the pillows and sighed. "No reason."

After the doctor left, I was alone with my thoughts and the television. Flipping through the channels reminded me how Walter liked to endlessly marvel at the options without choosing anything, which spawned another cycle of guilt and worry.

Where was my locket? When the doctor came in, I'd been so surprised she thought Ben hurt me, I forgot to ask.

Sitting up, I pushed the call button and waited for a nurse to appear. When the door opened, a kid walked in. Okay, fine, he was probably an adult given the nurse's scrubs, but he looked like Doogie Howser. Brown hair, brown eyes, white skin dotted with freckles, and a smile that made the whole place seem livelier.

"Hi, I'm Courtney," he said. "What do you need? Are you hungry? Dinner's in an hour, but I could look for snacks."

"Thanks, but no. Do you know what they did with my personal items when I came in? Car keys, wallet, jewelry?"

"Sure. It should be here," he said. "Is there something you need? I can grab it for you."

"I was wearing a heart-shaped locket on a chain. There are two pictures inside of a young woman and a man. The woman looks a lot like me."

"Is the guy your first crush?"

I snorted. "They're my grandparents."

"Ah. Usually, that stuff gets locked up. Let me check." A moment later, he returned with a sealed envelope. "It says this has your wallet and keys."

Taking the envelope, I held my breath, praying the outside label was incorrect. Unfortunately, it wasn't. Other than my wallet and key fob, the bag was empty.

"Maybe they didn't see it? Here are your clothes." He picked up a clear plastic bag from the chair in the corner.

The black yoga pants and royal blue zip-up sweatshirt I'd been wearing were clearly visible. Opening it up, I dug around inside. "Where's my shirt?"

"It, uh, got messed up," he said. "I think they threw it away, but I'll ask."

"Thanks. I might need something to wear home."

"The gift shop sells t-shirts. It might not be the most attractive, but it'll get the job done."

"Thanks. Can I go now?"

"That is a question for your doctor. I've got more patients to visit, but I'll check on you after dinner. If she gives the okay, I can take you down then. They're open late."

After Courtney left, I sat back to ponder my dilemma. When I placed the protection spells on my bedroom suite, I hadn't considered the possibility of needing to send someone into my closet to gather clothes. Theoretically, I could call a shirt to me, but the spell might not work at this range. Even if it did, there would be a lot of questions about clothing flying across town.

I'd have to find out if there was a way to temporarily lift the spell or give someone access.

Who would I ask? Dottie's number was in my ruined cell phone. Josie only knew kitchen magic. Maybe I could have her hold the phone up to Pink or Walter?

Or, since that was ridiculous, I could buy a shirt in the hospital's gift shop.

I resumed channel flipping, wishing I had my phone. Or my tablet. Without them, I felt completely isolated. My hospital room had a phone, so I could call someone, but how? The contact information for literally everyone I knew was in my phone. The only number I could recite from memory was the place Grandma Vera lived when I was nine. Did Information still exist? Could I dial 411?

The last time I tried, they didn't list cell phone numbers for privacy reasons. My mentor operated a massage therapy business, though. That number should be listed.

Turned out, I couldn't reach the bedside phone with all these tubes in me, anyway. I'd have to wait for someone to return and give it to me unless I used my magic to speed up the process.

My power took two forms. I was good with home and cleaning stuff: folding laundry was my specialty. But I also possessed ambient thread magic, which meant I could manipulate anything made of cloth. If anyone were within my range, I could bring them in here. The key was to do it subtly enough that they thought visiting me was their idea.

Closing my eyes, I leaned back and reached for my magic. Although I hadn't been using it, it seemed low, probably the result of the attack. My body was bruised and battered, and my magic had also taken a hit. Still, I was able to check a radius of about twenty feet on all sides.

On either side of my room, I found stiff, itchy cloth

similar to what I wore. More hospital gowns, probably. There was no need to disturb other patients, but maybe I could help. I reached out to the hospital gowns and bedsheets around me, sending calming thoughts and soothing emotions. After they warmed up to me, I asked them to release some of their stiffness. Instantly, everything around me relaxed.

Much better.

"I see you're making yourself right at home." The voice in the door made me jolt upright, embarrassed to be caught doing magic.

A woman in her mid-fifties with long dark hair and dancing blue eyes smiled at me. Immediately, my spirits lifted. "Olive! What are you doing here?"

Olive Green owned and operated the antique store in Shady Grove, not far from the bar. As someone born and raised in the small town, she must know the building's history. Considering I hadn't seen her since around Labor Day, her appearance felt like divine intervention.

"I found an object for you. When Aly touched it, she saw you getting thrown backward." Olive possessed psychic abilities and had trained our friend Aly to use hers. "Since we'd heard about the incident at the bar, it seemed best to bring this now."

To my immense relief, she held up a finely braided chain, from which dangled my heart-shaped locket.

"My necklace? How did you get it?"

"Aly found it in the street when she was on her way to get a latte. Her caffeine habit finally paid off."

"Oh, no. The vision didn't hurt her, did it? Is she okay?" The thought of my friend experiencing my pain, even though not my fault, made me wince.

"Aly is fine. She said you were attacked, but she didn't feel anything."

"Did she see what happened?"

"Something inside the bar growled or hissed at you. The sounds became louder, then the growling thing catapulted into you, followed by you hitting your head." Olive walked over and placed the locket in my palm. "Something burned right through the chain. You could've been seriously hurt."

"I am very grateful to be alive," I said. "Thank you so much for returning this. I wish Aly were here so I could thank her personally."

"She wanted to come, but she had to pick Kyle up from school." Aly moved to town to help her brother care for his young son, which meant lots of babysitting. "She'll text you later. May I sit?"

"After you returned my necklace, I'd bear a child for you. You have no idea how much it means to me." I paused. "Actually, I bet you do."

Her eyes twinkled. "I might have some idea. There's a lot of power stored in there."

Even though I couldn't wear the locket, the weight of it in my palm made me feel better. "It links me to my grandfather. I've been lost without it."

"After talking to Aly, I walked to the bar to look for anything out of the ordinary."

"And?"

She shook her head. "It was a normal, boarded-up building. Looked the same as every other time I walked by."

"Do you remember when the bar closed? Someone who worked there might be able to tell us who the ghost is."

"Oh, it happened ages ago. My Sam was a little boy, and he's got his MBA now." She thought for a moment. "The bar thrived when I was in high school, but I never went in. After

I turned twenty-one, my friends and I usually drove to Saratoga. It was more our scene. At some point, the owner —Leo Something—died."

"Who got the business? Was he married?"

"He was, but they were getting divorced. Leo's niece inherited it. Word was she wanted to do a big remodel; she hired contractors and everything. There were a couple of delays, but it was supposed to reopen around Halloween one year. Right before the big day, an early snowstorm took out the roof. We figured she couldn't afford to replace it. Poor thing disappeared."

"Does she still own the bar?"

"Oh, no. Over the years, it sold a few times. Things always went wrong. Failed health inspections, bank-ruptcies—once, lightning struck the front door! We feared the whole town would go up in flames. The owners had been running a ghost tour out of the building, and it seemed successful, but after that, they left town. No one else would touch the place. Eventually, someone boarded up the windows and posted foreclosure signs. All that's public record, so you can check my memory."

Public records wouldn't tell me if the niece killed Leo to inherit the bar. Or his wife, because murder seemed easier than a divorce. "Do you remember when it closed?"

"Sorry, dear, no. The *Shady Grove Sentinel* should have all this information in their archives. They would've run stories when Leo died and when the bar closed. The public library will have copies. For property records, I believe you have to visit Town Hall. Some of the larger areas have them online, but our mayor isn't interested in encouraging public access to knowledge."

I had so many questions about the mayor of Shady Grove, not least of which was: why did anyone vote for her?

Questions for another day. "Thanks, I guess. If only I had internet access, I'd check right now. Oh! I'll give you five thousand dollars for your phone."

"Nice try."

A groan escaped me. "Anything I can do without leaving this room?"

"Yes." She smiled at me. "Rest and recover."

"I was afraid you'd say that."

FOUR

The next morning, I awoke with a massive headache, sore ribs baffling modern medicine, and a fierce determination to get out of the hospital. Owning a bar was Ben's childhood dream, and he would not be stopped by a ghost. Not if I had anything to say about it.

Unfortunately, determination alone couldn't tell me how to evict a feline ghost from a commercial property. Should I bring in a ghost dog? Where would I even get a ghost dog?

Someone said my name, and I blinked several times, realizing what woke me: a man stood in the doorway. With effort, I shook my grogginess away. After Josie, Ben, and Olive, the number of people who knew to look for me here was fairly small. To my surprise, Willow Falls' only homicide detective, Timothy Pratt, stood in the doorway.

Tim was tall, in his mid-forties, with thick brown hair that had grayed at the temples and warm brown eyes. He reminded me of a younger Pierce Brosnan.

Since moving here, we'd run into each other several

times, mostly because I kept finding dead people. Not my fault, but it caused problems, especially when I'd spent so much time lying about my unlikely knowledge of each victim. Still, we shared a mutual attraction and were working on building trust. Over the past few months, we'd developed a friendship that might be a path to more. Taking things slow was fine with me, after the last guy I liked tried to kill me.

The sight of him instantly raised my spirits. "Aren't you out of your jurisdiction, Detective? The attack happened in Shady Grove."

When he moved toward the bed, concern shone in his brown eyes. His eyes roved over the hospital bed, looking for injuries. I took advantage of the silence to drink in his appearance. I might have been a teenager when Pierce Brosnan starred as Bond, but I'd had as big a crush on 007 as anyone.

When he seemed satisfied I wasn't mortally wounded, Tim met my eyes. "The Shady Grove Sheriff's Department only has two full-time officers. Smallest one in the state. They call me to back them up from time to time. Their deputy is moving this week, so the Sheriff called me. I live much closer to the hospital than he does."

"Well, it's nice to see you."

"I would prefer other circumstances, but I know what you mean." He gestured at the empty chair beside my bed. "Mind if I sit?"

"Not at all. I imagine you have some questions about yesterday."

"You're right. I'm hoping your answers don't involve any dead bodies."

"I did not see any dead bodies," I said. That was true. My brain hadn't quite wrapped itself around the idea of ghosts existing in species other than human, and even if a ghost had attacked me, there was no deceased human in the vicinity.

"What an oddly specific way of phrasing things."

"I never made it inside. After decades of being vacant, the bar could contain anything."

"Touché." He pulled out his ever-present notepad and pen. Tim didn't believe in relying on electronics to keep his notes. Writing it all down helped him think. "What were you doing at the bar?"

"You know Ben Cartwright, right?"

"Don't tell me you and Ben were going for drinks? Surely you knew the building's been abandoned for decades."

I wanted to ask if his voice carried a note of jealousy, but let it go. "Ben wants to buy the bar, and he asked me to investigate the rumors."

"Ah, yes. The rumors." His eyes met mine squarely. "Rumors like the ones about you."

"Not entirely dissimilar," I agreed. Tim had gotten a demonstration of my abilities when capturing the person who murdered Ben's stepfather, so there was no need to be sly. "We went to look around. Unfortunately, what happened can't go in your report."

He sighed. "That is a dilemma. What do you suggest?"

"Ben and I are friends. Say I accompanied him as a fellow small business owner. Or say I was too medicated to give you a coherent explanation, but I remember falling. That's somewhat true."

His lips twitched. "You seem pretty lucid to me. What happened?"

Step-by-step, I took him through everything I remembered, without editing. Once he knew, he'd figure out how to phrase the report.

"We're saying I lost my balance," I finished.

"What about Walter?"

"He's at the mansion, but you can't interview a ghost. Your witnesses are me and Ben. I fell. Case closed. Nothing to interest the police."

"I'm glad to hear it, I think." He paused. "I don't like the idea of you putting yourself in danger."

"That wasn't intentional. The other ghosts I've met, if not entirely pleasant, at least said hello. I never thought any of them would hurt me. To be honest, I didn't know a ghost *could* attack."

"Fair enough," he said. "But we both know you're going back in. Can I convince you to take precautions?"

"If you're asking if I'm willing to avoid a second hospital trip, absolutely."

"Glad we're on the same page." Our eyes met, and my pulse quickened. Even though this wasn't a social visit, it was nice to have him here.

"First, I need to do some research. A friend was here earlier, giving me background on the building, but she can't see ghosts. If the bar is haunted, I need to know by who. Why? How did he or she get the power to influence the outside world? Until we find some answers, I'm not going anywhere near the bar."

NOT LONG AFTER TIM LEFT, Dr. Lopez announced I would be released by lunchtime.

Immediately, I called Josie. "I'll give you ten thousand dollars to come get me."

She laughed. "Your money is no good here. Give me a time, and I'm there. Or I can ask T to do it while I make lunch. He'll jump at the chance to drive your car again."

Until she'd mentioned it, I'd forgotten asking Ben to have T pick up my Porsche and return it to the mansion. "Did my girl make it in one piece?"

"Other than a brief incident with T insisting he needed to sleep in your car to 'keep her safe,' everything is fine." She lowered her voice. "He's worried, Emma. We couldn't tell him what happened, even if we wanted to."

Guilt washed over me. T had arrived at my place shortly after I moved to Willow Falls. His parents kicked him out, and Olive recommended he stay with me while he figured out what he wanted to do. Josie and I welcomed him, but he was a normal teenaged kid. Neither of us mentioned the ghosts, the talking cat, or magic.

"What did you say?"

"I made it sound like a minor heart attack. Told Ben not to correct him unless or until you gave the okay."

"A heart attack might make me stagger backward and fall," I said. "Sounds legit."

"Talk to T," she said gently. "He won't betray your secret."

I heaved a heavy sigh, but she was right. People in small towns loved to gossip, and it would be a miracle if T hadn't already heard the rumors about me. The boy had eyes, ears, and a brain between them. He definitely noticed things; he just didn't mention them. When his parents turned on him, he'd been looking for someone to trust. How could I be that person while maintaining a lie?

T had such a good head on his shoulders, part of me

worried he'd run screaming if I started talking about magic and ghosts. Part of me feared he'd refuse to leave the hospital with me until I got a brain scan. But maybe if I wanted him to trust me, I should trust him first.

The lanky teenager waited in my car when the nurse wheeled me out to the curb. I'd insisted I was perfectly capable of walking, but she said something about hospital liability, so I let it go.

Until seeing my friend in the driver's seat, I hadn't realized it went back that far. He was over six feet tall, ate like a horse, and never gained an ounce. He wore his coarse black hair cropped close when we'd met, but he'd let it grow.

When I opened the passenger-side door, T beamed at me. His excitement at being allowed to drive shone through. "You don't mind if I drive, right?"

"Nope. They're releasing me, but I still feel like a horse kicked me in the chest."

"Ouch. Do you need to stop anywhere? Take a quick detour up to Montreal? In this sweet ride, I will take you wherever you want to go."

I laughed, but his question made me think.

My first instinct should have been to go home and check on Walter, but I felt naked without my cell phone. The hospital was on the far side of town, nearly twenty minutes from my home. I could ask T to take me to the mansion, talk to my grandfather, then head back, but it made more sense to buy a phone now.

Practicality won out. Josie had already given everyone an update on my condition. They knew the hospital had released me. Another hour wouldn't make a difference. Besides, I needed to see if my old phone uploaded anything to the cloud in the split second between me approaching the bar and getting attacked. Maybe the footage would provide a clue.

As soon as I got buckled, I asked T to take me to the nearest phone store. When I told the salesman I wanted to pay cash for a new phone with zero discussion, he looked delighted. The entire transaction took less than ten minutes. Before we left the store, I'd already logged into the cloud and was watching everything download.

Back in the car, the device was in my hand before I realized, if the video showed what I expected, watching it in front of a non-magical teen would raise a lot of questions. Josie's words came back to me.

I took a deep breath. It was time.

"What's wrong?" T asked. "Are you okay? Is the car okay?"

His concern made me laugh. Laughing hurt my ribs, and I winced. A long moment passed before I said, "I'm fine. There's just, uh, something I have to tell you. I didn't have a heart attack."

"Considering that you and Ben tried to exorcise the bar, I'm not shocked to hear that."

His words made my mouth drop open. "You knew about that? You believe in ghosts?"

"I've heard the rumors, Emma. Even back home in Troy, everyone knows the Shady Grove bar is haunted. It was even in the papers. A bunch of my friends came up to see it a couple of years ago. People have *also* said they think your mansion is haunted." He paused. "It's not just ghost stuff, though. The house is always spotless, your clothes never wrinkle or get dirty, and last month when I spilled coffee on the couch, the stain vanished before you got home. Either you hit the jackpot with a ghost that loves to clean, or you're a witch."

My face grew warm. "Josie warned me about that spell. I swore no one would notice."

"I may be eighteen, but I'm not stupid."

"Never thought you were," I assured him. "Just got a little overconfident."

"You could have told me, you know."

"I'm sorry. The Magical Enforcement Office—wait, am I allowed to mention them? Oops. Anyway, they insisted there would be dire consequences if word got out. But I should have trusted you."

"You're letting me drive your car. That is the ultimate act."

"One of two," I said. "I'm going to watch the video of what happened at the bar. You might be about to see something unbelievable."

"Or I might see something that makes perfect sense," he said. "I've seen magic before."

"You know about Josie?" I asked in surprise.

The words came out before I realized that if she hadn't told him, I did. Then again, she was the reason I began this conversation.

He grinned widely. "I suspected about Josie. There's something about her food. Her hot cocoa makes me twice as happy as the powdered mix."

"That's not magic," I said. "That's milk. The powder makes hot brown water."

"But *in addition*, if you'd told me about your powers earlier, I would have mentioned the secret of my green thumb." He held up one hand and wiggled his fingers, his eyes never leaving the road. "It's not love."

"I knew it! You have magic with plants," I accused him.

"Guilty." His face turned serious. "Now watch that

video. I need to know if you caught a ghost on camera. Do you know how many views we can get on TikTok?"

"Don't you dare."

The video opened with a shot of the front doors. The only sounds were my feet on the ground and Ben's voice behind me, urging me to be careful.

Suddenly, the camera lens jerked upward. A blur of light flashed by. Then the screen went dark. That was it. I tried to slow it down, zoom in, but nothing made a difference. I couldn't get the blur to clear, and it never appeared like anything other than a lightning bolt on an otherwise clear, cloudless day.

The video hadn't captured a single clue.

FIVE

"Emma!!!!!!!!" Walter's joy at seeing me step out of the car nearly bowled me over. A peal of laughter escaped me as he bolted through a top-floor window and floated to the ground. "Are you okay? Do you need me to kick some ghostly buttocks? When are we going back to the bar? I've been practicing my jujitsu."

He busted out a few moves. It did, indeed, look like he'd learned some tricks from YouTube.

T paused, halfway out of the passenger side. "You okay? Because you're acting like you hit your head harder than they thought. I could keep the car so it's safe."

"Nice try," I said. "Walter's happy to see me back in one piece."

He shook his head. "I suspected you talked to ghosts, but it's somehow weirder *knowing* there's half a conversation I can't hear."

"No. With Walter, the whole conversation is usually weirder."

My grandfather huffed but smiled to let me know he didn't mind.

To him, I said, "I'm sorry! When I got attacked, the necklace came off. I got it back, though."

"You should put a homing spell on it," he said as we headed into the house.

"I don't think I can."

"Why not? You've got magic tied to the home! Set it to return here instantly if it comes off your neck. A safe place, like inside your trunk."

Never had it occurred to me that such a thing might be possible. Over the past few months, I'd become very familiar with Walter's spell books and mine, but his book had an infuriating habit of hiding spells it didn't think I was ready for. "That's brilliant. I'll look into it. Thanks."

The front door opened, and Josie stepped onto the porch. My dark-haired friend used to hunch when she walked, but since coming here, she held her head high. Her once-sallow brown skin glowed. Living here without fear of her ex-husband and developing her kitchen magic agreed with her. "There you are! Lunch is waiting. I hope you're hungry."

"Starving," T and I said in unison.

Before eating, I wanted to fix my locket. When we found it in the basement, the locket hung on the same delicate chain Walter had purchased when presenting it to Grandma Vera. While it wouldn't take long to order another chain from the local jewelry store, I had a better idea.

But when Josie insisted it was time to stop with the magic and eat, she meant it. I'd made it two steps toward the staircase when she grabbed my shoulders and steered me toward the kitchen door. "You've been in the hospital. Rest. Eat."

"Yes, *Mom*," I teased.

In response, she pointed at the door. I ducked my head

and went to see what she'd made. The array of food made my jaw drop.

True to her word, Josie had prepared a feast for my return. The table sagged under the weight of a tray of enchiladas, a BBQ chicken pizza, an entire roasted chicken, pulled pork, chicken lo mein, and a platter of hamburgers.

"Is the army coming to lunch?" I asked.

She blushed. "I wasn't sure what you wanted, so I made a bit of everything."

"I appreciate that, but it'll take weeks to eat all this."

"Speak for yourself," T said, moving past me to pull out a chair.

"See?" Josie said. "We have a teenager in the house. It'll be gone before you know it."

"Uh-huh. I love you, too." I hugged her for a long moment before turning back to the table.

After we stuffed ourselves with the delicious mountain of food, I excused myself. Up in my room, I dug in my trunk for a thick, white silken cord. Any spells involving cloth or fabric worked better on fibers I'd woven myself. This cord required many silkworm-collecting trips into the woods. At the time, it seemed tedious, but Pink assured me it would be worth it, and he'd been right.

Now, I unraveled about a foot of the silk and asked it to separate from the spool. Grandma Vera's locket slid over the end before the cord fastened itself around my neck, weaving the ends together so seamlessly it was impossible to tell where the circle connected.

A glance in the mirror showed it hanging exactly where the last one had been. Perfect. The magic hummed against my skin, as if saying it was proud of me. I was pretty proud of myself, too.

Before heading down, I pulled Walter's spell book out

of my trunk. Near the back, on a page I would've sworn used to be blank, was a homing spell. A quick scan of the words showed it was relatively straightforward, and it only took a moment to say the words. If my locket came off my neck again, it should teleport to the trunk immediately. No more worrying about losing something so important.

In the bottom of my trunk, my great-great-grandmother's grimoire lay wrapped in a protective cloth. Pulling it out, I gently removed the fabric, marveling at how well-preserved everything was. Then I ran my fingers over the letters on the front: *Property of Evelyn Sparrow*. My touch deactivated the protective spell keeping her secrets safe, allowing the book to fall open.

Evelyn was a powerful memory witch. Her book wouldn't even consider letting me see most of the pages yet. She also had a lot of useful general purpose spells, and that's what I needed right now. I flipped through, looking for anything to bind an unfriendly spirit or place a protective spell around the bar. These spells were older than me, most of them older than Walter. I didn't have the power to work them all, and the one I did a few months ago wiped me out for more than a day, but I had to try.

About a third of the way in, I found a protection spell that should work. Digging into the trunk again, I pulled out a few ingredients. A quick trip to the garden should get me the other things I needed. T kept it well-stocked, and his magic explained why so many non-native plants thrived despite the season.

Now that I was ready to return to the bar, I took the book to the ballroom where Walter spent most of his time. The earlier discussion about my locket had distracted me from asking what he saw before the attack.

Walter floated near the piano, looking out the massive

windows at the grounds. The property spanned several acres, most of them wooded. Behind the house, there were two small cottages, a pool house, the (currently unusable) pool, and a barn that would eventually be converted to a garage. Probably after my first New York winter hit. Or possibly during.

He clapped when I showed him the improvements to my necklace. "Getting bounced back here is very disorienting, you know."

"I can imagine," I said. "I feel terrible. It shouldn't happen again."

He let out a huff, but the corners of his eyes twinkled before his face turned serious. "You scared me back there. You never said talking to a ghost was dangerous."

"That's what I wanted to talk to you about. It shouldn't have been. Or at least, I didn't know it might be. I thought ghosts couldn't interact with the human world other than talking to me. You can't move items, right? Or attack people?"

"Why would I attack anyone?"

"Hypothetically. If you wanted to swat a fly off my arm, could you?"

"No." Pink trotted past me and hopped onto the piano bench before turning around to face us. "It is very unusual to encounter a ghost who manipulates objects."

"Have you seen it before?" I asked. "How does it happen?"

"Yeah! I want to do that," Walter said. "Not the attacking thing. But I'd love to play catch again. Or eat enchiladas. Mmm, enchiladas!"

"What you might be dealing with," Pink said, "is a manifest spirit controlled by a talisman. Usually, a manifest spirit is solid, and their actions are directed by the witch who created them. You'd have to find and destroy the talisman."

This seemed much more daunting than a normal haunted building.

"What about a regular ghost? Is it possible for them to touch things?"

Pink said, "I've only encountered it once, many years ago. In that case, the ghost had been dead for an extended time."

"Like me!" Walter shouted. "Teach me!"

"It's not that simple. First, I'm not a ghost. I wouldn't have the first idea how to teach you. When I want to touch something, I touch it." Pink illustrated his point by stepping on the piano keys. Something thudded, and he winced. "You should get this tuned."

"Top of my to-do list," I said dryly. "What's extended? I'm not sure when the bar shut down, but it sounds like it's only been about twenty years."

"Maybe no one knew the ghost was there. If they couldn't or didn't want to make themselves known, a spirit can go undetected. Maybe the business shut down because they revealed themself."

It might take time to dig through the old *Shady Grove Sentinel* archives to review every death over the past forty years, but... No, but, actually. That sounded dreadful.

I sighed. "Could a ghost who hangs around for decades be someone who passed naturally, or am I looking for an unexplained death?"

"Didn't you feel the rage?" Walter said. "No way that person died of natural causes. They were furious."

"You saw a person?" I asked.

"When you got hit? No, I was enjoying the sunshine. I assumed we were dealing with a human spirit."

"I know this will sound weird, but I thought it was a cat's ghost."

Pink snorted. "Oh, you're serious? That's very interesting."

"Interesting, sure. How does she investigate every cat who died thirty years ago?" Walter asked.

"You shouldn't have to," Pink said. "My guess is the cat is protecting someone else. It is very unusual for an animal to become a ghost. They need strong ties to a human unless magic is involved."

"So I'm looking for a person connected with the bar who had a cat and died a long time before the first reported haunting?" The longer Pink spoke, the more impossible the situation seemed.

"If anyone can do it, you can," Walter said. "I have faith in you."

"Are there other possibilities? Something that doesn't require months of research?"

"It might be a residual haunting," Pink said.

"A residential haunting? Isn't that what I have *here*? In the mansion."

He shook his head. "Residual. When something very traumatic, like a murder, happens, the victim can leave their emotions on the space."

"What about Martha? She was murdered, and she didn't leave any residue in the kitchen."

"Martha was an exceptionally logical and grounded person. In a residual haunting, the spirit usually has strong emotional ties to the living or the space where the event happened. Martha's strongest tie was to her late husband."

Walter said, "She was weird. Completely fine with being dead."

"Like I said, exceptionally grounded." If a cat could look smug, Pink did.

I asked, "How do we clear a residual haunting?"

"One of the easier options is to discover what caused the ghost's distress and resolve it," Pink said. "With a murder, find the killer, like with Darren."

"Right. So, I need to find out if anyone died at the bar under suspicious circumstances," I said. "How? Look up prior owners in the property records, search old newspaper articles? Talk to people who lived around here twenty years ago?"

Walter cleared his throat. "This whole research thing sounds like a lot of trouble. If you want to know who the ghost is, why don't we ask them?"

"Brilliant! I don't know why I didn't think of that!" I slapped my forehead with one palm, then glowered at him. "It put me in the hospital, remember?"

"You, not me," he retorted. "I was fine. You waltzed in like we owned the place. We didn't have a right to be there, and the occupants knew it."

"Ben is interested in buying the building. He had permission to go in and look around before deciding. Technically, we had more right to be there than the ghost."

Pink smirked. "Be sure to tell them that from a safe distance."

"I'm glad you're so amused." To Walter, I said, "What are you proposing?"

"Let's go back. You and me. Leave Ben behind. Park down the street. We'll walk up, nice and slow. I'll go ahead, and maybe the ghost will agree to a little parlay."

"It could be dangerous."

"Or it could be the most exciting thing I've done in

almost thirty years. I've sat back and watched you have all the fun since you arrived. You owe me."

Poor Walter. He'd been so lonely and bored before I moved in. Not that boredom was a good reason to let a loved one risk their life, but I understood why he wanted to help.

"Can they hurt him?" I asked Pink.

"Nothing can hurt him. He's dead. Your other option is to sift through decades of obituaries."

Grabbing my keys, I headed for the door. "Come on."

SIX

When I was three steps from the front door, Ben appeared on the porch as if he were the one with magic. "Where do you think you're going?"

I skidded to a halt. My cheeks burned. "Back to the bar. I can't let anyone else get hurt."

"Anyone else like you?" Ben crossed his arms and shouted toward the kitchen. "Josie! I got her!"

My friend appeared in the doorway, and I stuck my tongue out at her. "Traitor."

"As soon as Ben explained what happened, I knew you'd head right back over there. Didn't anyone ever teach you to heed a warning?"

"No, they taught me to take care of others. Look, I'm not going in. The bar is haunted. Walter never made it across the street. We're going back to see if this ghost is open to speaking with someone who isn't living. We know they've got at least one thing in common."

"Our snappy sense of style?" Walter said, gesturing. Until that moment, I hadn't realized he'd changed into a beige jumpsuit. On his back, he wore something that looked like the proton packs out of *Ghostbusters*.

I smiled at him, but Josie wasn't budging. She and Ben blocked both exits. The only way out was through the ballroom or Josie's bedroom, both of which would put me in the backyard, giving my friends plenty of time to block my car.

A heavy sigh escaped me. "What's it going to take to get you to let me go? I promise not to try anything unless the ghost seems open to communication. I'll wait in the car. Walter can cross the street without me."

"You make me sound like a kindergartner. I've been crossing streets since before you were born," he grumbled. "Tell them to let you go or you'll have Pink leave a surprise in their beds."

Since I would do no such thing, I ignored him. Instead, I met Josie's gaze with a piercing stare. "Don't make me move you out of the way."

"You wouldn't lay a hand on her," Ben said.

Josie snorted. "She wouldn't have to. Witch, remember?"

The blood drained out of Ben's face.

"She knows I wouldn't do it. But come on. What if an innocent person approaches that bar and gets hurt? It's between two open businesses. They may have the sidewalk roped off, but that won't stop everyone. I need to protect the area."

After a long pause, Josie threw up her hands. "Okay, fine. You've got me. Recon only. Send Walter in to scout the premises and wait for him to report back. If you enter that bar on your own, you'll be serving buttered Pop-Tarts to your guests for the next month."

Ben shuddered. "For my sake, please, don't go inside."

"Deal. Come on, Walter. Let's go before they change their minds."

After a quick trip into the garden to gather sage for the protection spell, we got in the car and headed toward Shady Grove.

Before we left, I showed Walter the video I took yesterday. Then we reviewed everything we remembered from our first visit. The thought of being able to affect things got him extremely excited.

"Did you ever see the movie *Ghost*?" he asked. "Patrick Swayze met that spirit on the subway who taught him to channel his rage into moving things."

I shot him a sideways glance. "Don't take this the wrong way, but you are the least rage-filled person I've ever met. Can you channel happier emotions, like unbridled joy or childlike wonder?"

He folded his arms and huffed, but a smile crept onto his face. "Now you're flattering me."

"It's not my fault you're delightful." I parked near the coffee shop rather than in front of the bar. Maybe if we approached from the side, slowly, things would go better. "Can you make it inside without me moving?"

"There's only one way to find out, isn't there? Don't tell me you're scared. Not after all the things you said to Ben and Josie."

"Scared isn't the word. I'd rather only get smashed in the chest and tossed into the street once this week, especially because you can't call 911. I'm better off waiting here."

Walter moved across my lap to the driver's side door. I closed my eyes so I couldn't see him. Even after all these months, the image of him partially in and partially out of objects—or me!—made me queasy. Unfortunately, my reaction amused him, so I was trying to get used to it. Or at least hide my discomfort.

"Good luck," I said.

"Don't need it," he retorted through the glass. "Just keep your necklace on."

In response, I stuck my tongue out at him before rolling down the window to listen.

Stillness filled the air. This area would be busy later in the day, but we were weeks outside of tourist season, and most residents were at school or work. Whether the lack of activity near the bar meant the ghost didn't know we were here or wanted to meet my grandfather, I didn't know. He might be napping.

Last time, the wind didn't spring up until we tried to get out of the car. If I opened my door, would the ghost slam it shut?

Walter moved confidently across the street and onto the sidewalk. I tilted my head, trying to hear anything but chirping birds and music from the coffee shop.

There it was. A low growl, like before. It was on the tip of my tongue to remind Walter to be careful, but if the ghost hadn't noticed me, I didn't want to alert him to my presence. We still didn't know how far it could stray beyond the bar's perimeter.

Barely had I finished the thought when Walter turned toward me and hollered. "Hey, Emma! I don't see anything!"

Oh, for Pete's sake.

I got out and moved into the middle of the street, hissing, "Don't you know what it means to be stealthy?"

"Sorry. I got out of practice, being dead and all. No one ever notices me except you."

The growl behind him grew louder, showing the falsity

of the words. The spirit occupying the bar had noticed him. Judging by the sounds, it wasn't pleased to meet another ghost.

Walter whirled around, unlocking the blaster or whatever from his backpack. Waving it before him like a wand, he crouched down and took one small step at a time toward the yellow tape across the sidewalk. When he reached it, he didn't even pause. A step from the entrance, the caramel-and-white blur from yesterday burst through the door. He was massive, far bigger than your ordinary house cat. Given the fluffiness, I guessed he'd once been a Maine Coon.

What originally blended into one color in my memory was actually a mostly white body dotted with caramel, a brown face, and two paws in each color. He had a kink in his caramel-colored tail, as if attacking me wasn't his first fight. When alive, this must've been a gorgeous cat. Scruffy, but gorgeous. Part of me wanted to reach out and stroke his luxurious-looking fur to see if my hand passed through him. Then I remembered my prior visit and quelled the urge.

Instinctively, I backed up. The cat fell to the ground, shaking his head.

"Hello, there," Walter said, crouching down. "Good kitty."

The cat growled and swiped at his outstretched hand. Walter let out a yelp. "He scratched me! How did he scratch me?"

"I don't know, but get out of there before he does worse."

He stepped backward. "We don't want to hurt you. We just want to go inside and look around."

The cat bared his teeth. This wasn't working.

We retreated to my car, and Walter showed me his

hand. It appeared to be oozing, the same way a regular, non-magical wound bled. "I haven't been injured in twenty-six years! How did he do that?"

"I have no idea, but we are clearly not welcome here." Although the cat hadn't ventured more than a few feet from the bar door, he didn't seem bound by any rules I knew. If he jumped into my car, we'd be in big trouble. "Let me put up some protections, and then we'll go."

With Great-Great-Grandma's book in hand, I lit the incense and waved it in a circle. The sage was supposed to go in the corners of the bar, but that was impossible. I inched toward the middle of the street, tossing it when it seemed unwise to go any closer. Hopefully, no one saw me crouching in the middle of the street, sprinkling spices on the ground while chanting.

After making it back to relative safety beside the car, I focused my attention on the building and uttered words to prevent anyone from walking toward the bar. Similar to the wards on my bedroom at home, anyone intent on visiting should feel an uncontrollable desire to go anywhere else.

Normally, when I performed a spell, the magic moved through me. The power flowed, becoming almost tangible. Right now, I felt nothing. "Did it work?"

"I can't tell," Walter said. "I've had a powerful urge to be elsewhere since the cat scratched me."

Lightning flashed. The sky opened, and rain crashed down around us. Walter looked up and cackled, drinking it all in. I dove inside the car so my precious spell book wouldn't get destroyed. While my grandfather danced in the rain, I read the spell again.

A moment later, Walter joined me. "What happened?"

"It looks like I did everything right," I said. "I don't know why it didn't work."

"Maybe something much more powerful than you is protecting the bar and doesn't want your interference."

"Exactly. We should get out of here."

"Let's try again," he suggested. "Bring some catnip with us. Oh! Let's go to the pet store and borrow a dog to chase him away."

I put on my seatbelt and started the car without responding. "First, I'm pretty sure the pet store doesn't loan animals. Second, how would we convince a dog to chase a ghost?"

"Dogs see ghosts."

"What? Really?"

"Sure. Don't you ever notice they bark when nothing's there? Ghosts."

To be honest, I wasn't sure ghosts answered that question, but it didn't matter. Pink would never allow a dog in his domain.

"What do we do now?" I mused while pulling out of the space. The moment we turned the corner, the rain stopped. "This is bananas. I promised Ben I would help. Everything I try gets shut down. This thing is way bigger than me. I don't know how to move forward."

Walter said, "Maybe he should open something a little less dangerous, like a nice axe-throwing club."

SEVEN

The trip home began in silence while I pondered what happened and Walter examined his fresh wound from all angles.

"Have you ever heard of a ghost having a pet?" I finally asked.

"What, you think we have monthly mixers? I don't know any more ghosts than you do."

Touché.

"Sorry. You have Pink, right?"

"He's not a pet. Pink was with me most of my life; he disappeared when I died. He said he had other people to help before my heir arrived. He seemed to know when you would appear, but I didn't ask how."

This was so frustrating. I was a witch! I should be able to use magic to solve problems. Unfortunately, thread magic against a ghost was useless. Hearth magic was great for cleaning the house in a snap or changing the wallpaper, but nothing I'd ever experienced prepared me for this.

What a bust.

Maybe the bar should remain closed. Ben hadn't paid

the tax lien yet. He could take his money somewhere else and leave the bar empty until a better witch showed up.

"Hey. I know that look on your face," Walter said. "Everything is going to be okay."

"I got you attacked by a ghost. You're actually injured."

"Look at the bright side. Now we know that's possible. Information is power."

He had a point. Maybe, before I gave up, I should do the research we'd been avoiding: who owned the bar, did they have pets, and whether anyone died there under mysterious circumstances. If the prior owner(s) still lived in the area, we needed to talk to them.

When we passed the turn for the road leading to the mansion, Walter jumped. "Hey! That's us. Did you forget where we live?"

I shook my head. "Not yet. We've got one more stop first."

"What?"

"I believe you called it 'that boring research thing' earlier."

He let out a groan. "Can you take off the necklace again?"

A chuckle escaped me. "It won't be that bad. But I can't let you go—I might need you. Back in the late '80s and early '90s, you were the most popular guy in town. Everyone knew you. Once we know who to talk to, you can tell me all about them."

He crossed his arms and looked out the window, but he wore a smug smile. As dreadful as reading old newspapers sounded to my grandfather, he appreciated being needed. "What's the first step? Property records?"

"Nah. We'd have to go back to Shady Grove for those. I'll

check next time we're there. For now, I thought we'd start with old newspapers."

Shady Grove didn't have its own public library due to the low population. That shouldn't have come as a surprise; after all, they had zero bars. Residents who wanted to check out a book without driving to Saratoga had their choice between the campus library at nearby Maloney College, or the Willow Falls Public Library, about three miles from my house. I chose the latter.

The stately library took up an entire block, with two stories made of stone with a massive staircase leading up to the front. Carved pillars flanked the double doors, which must be at least twelve feet high. It reminded me of something out of a story.

The airy interior lifted my mood. Tall shelves holding rows of books stretched as far as the eye could see. Floor-to-ceiling windows in the double-high walls filled the room with natural light.

"This place is amazing!" Walter yelled. The words echoed. "—zing, ing, ing..."

"Shh," I said automatically. "It's a library. We have to be quiet."

"Oh, hush yourself. No one hears me, and this is the most beautiful place I've been in ages. Look at the high ceilings, the enormous windows, that curved staircase—and books! So many books! I bet there's even one about talking to the dead."

"Why do I need a book? I already talk to the dead."

"Did it ever occur to you that I might want to talk to someone other than you and that cat? I miss Toby." My next-door neighbor had been a few decades younger than Walter, but they'd grown close toward the end of his life.

"I'm sorry." My grandfather embraced each day with

such glee, sometimes I forgot how lonely he was. "Let's get what we came for, and if there's time, we'll explore. If not, we'll come back."

"You get what we came for. I'm exploring now." Before I could utter another word, my grandfather sailed away, leaving me bemused in the lobby.

What now?

How did a cat become a ghost? I'd only been able to see ghosts for a few months, but all were human. It seemed like, if there were animal ghosts in addition to human ghosts, I should see both. Or if I couldn't, then why could I see *this particular* cat ghost?

After browsing the library's suspiciously large section on the occult, I picked up two non-fiction tomes dealing with hauntings and spirits to flip through at home. Pink would have insight, but I needed a foundation to know what to ask.

Then I turned my attention to the bar's history. Maybe there had been an incident involving the death of a cat. When we'd walked in, I'd spotted an entire wall near the entrance covered with multiple newspapers and maga-zines. Unfortunately, when I returned to that section, they didn't have anything recent. A sign informed me that all periodicals from 2015 on could be searched using the library's computers.

Two thousand fifteen was more than ten years after the bar shut down permanently. The articles stored on the computer wouldn't help. Nothing told me where to find older issues of the paper, so I headed for the Reference Desk.

A smiling Black woman about ten years older than me with large red glasses and a long gray braid down her back sat behind the circulation desk. She looked delighted to see me, as if she didn't get many people passing through. I hoped that wasn't true.

Public libraries were one of my favorite places when I was a kid: the land of escape, where I could be anyone, travel anywhere. At first, it was a way of getting out of the house when my mom didn't want me around. Then Grandma Vera brought me every Saturday after I moved in with her and Grandpa Ed.

The librarian happily directed me to the back issues of the *Shady Grove Sentinel*. "It's so exciting to help someone research! No one ever asks to look at these, you know."

Considering that she'd led me to what appeared to be an old card catalog next to some kind of overhead projector, it wasn't shocking that people didn't dig through this stuff more often. Clouds of dust would probably shoot out of those tiny drawers when opened.

As if reading my mind, the librarian laughed, not unkindly. "I know it's daunting, but it's simple to use once you know how. Here, I'll show you."

"Isn't this stuff online now?"

"Maybe in larger communities. We've put current editions in the computer for the past eight years, but there's no budget to go back and add the older papers. It's not a priority. Anyone who wants old news reads the *New York Times* archives."

"Do you have those online?" I asked hopefully.

She shook her head ruefully. "We couldn't afford the subscription. Maybe someday. You could get a consumer one, probably a lot cheaper."

"Remind me to make a big donation to the library when I get home."

"Yeah, right. Sounds great. If you need anything, my name's Consuela." Muttering to herself, she walked away.

She clearly didn't believe me about the donation, but I meant it.

Although the machine appeared to be older than me, using it was fairly straightforward. Find the dates I needed on the front of the massive card catalog-looking thing, pull out the box of film, load it. Turn on the light in the machine, lean forward into the eyepiece, and scroll.

The computer on top of the storage unit told me which boxes held mentions of the bar and Leo West, but not what those mentions were. I had to pull a dozen boxes and go through them one at a time.

An hour later, I knew all about the Shady Grove Annual Treasure Hunt, established and sponsored by my grandfather; the fundraisers used to build Town Hall; why Shady Grove got to be in its own county (I still didn't fully understand, but I knew the official reason); when famous soap opera actress Thelma Reyes moved to town; and that *Sentinel* reporter Hal Crews was named Shady Grove Citizen of the Year in 2002.

The newspaper also told me when the bar opened, but reported no mysterious deaths in the years immediately before or after. Besides that, I found the notice when Leo filed for divorce and his obituary, which said he died of a heart attack. No ghost mentions.

"Did you know there's an entire room of toys up there?"

When Walter's voice popped up out of nowhere, I jerked and almost stabbed myself with the eyepiece. He'd been roaming the library for so long, I'd forgotten he was here. "A children's room? I guess that makes sense."

"It's amazing. They have books and puzzles and trains! Oh, I used to love trains." He clasped his hands to his chest. "Trains are so much fun. When we get this ghost talking to us, can you ask him or her to teach me to manipulate objects? It would be so much fun to play with trains again."

Poor Walter. In the past few weeks, I'd introduced him to the wonders of streaming TV, but he still wasn't really a part of the world. "We can ask. I don't know what they'll say, but how about, when all this is resolved, you and I go for a train ride?"

"Yes!" He clapped several times. "Thank you, thank you!"

Normally this would be the perfect time for a hug, but of course, such a thing was impossible. I smiled. "It'll be nice to take a trip together, but for now, we have more research to do."

"On that? That thing's ancient. It looks like something they used back when I was alive. I thought you said the twenty-first century made good technology."

"Astounding technological advances have been made in the past twenty years," I said. "However, this might be the machine used during your lifetime. They're in desperate need of upgrades. Give me ten minutes to see what else I can find. So far, it's nothing but dead ends."

After picking up and loading another reel, I leaned forward again to look through the viewfinder.

This time, Walter's voice came from inside the machine. "What am I supposed to be looking at?"

"Did you walk into the projector?"

"No! Don't be ridiculous. I stuck my head in so we could read together. Thought it might help, but all I see is gray."

"You're probably looking at the inside of a metal box," I said. This wasn't going to work. It would be better to come back later. "Get out of there. I'll finish as fast as I can."

Instead, he moved around and slid into my seat—with me in it. Even though I couldn't feel him, goosebumps rose on my arms. To resume reading articles, I'd have to put my head through his. The thought made me shudder. "Please move. You know it freaks me out when we occupy the same space."

"Fine." He slid to one side. "You better read me everything you see. And I want a train ride as soon as possible."

"Yes, sir."

"Hold on." I stopped scrolling. "We may have something. The *Shady Grove Sentinel*, 'Local Businessman Missing,' from 2002."

"What does it say?"

"On Wednesday evening, the Shady Grove Sheriff's Department received a call that local businessman Miles Levine, 26, had not reported to work and might be in danger. Levine worked as the manager at Two Mules, the Second Street bar undergoing renovations. The bar closed last year following the death of its prior owner. 'He was always punctual,' bar owner Lucky Risk, 24, reported. 'We often spoke throughout the day. When he didn't check in by lunch, I grew concerned. I called the bar, but no one answered. His cell phone went to voice mail.' When questioned, the neighboring business owners had not seen or heard from Levine. His car was not in the employee parking lot behind the building."

"According to Lucky, the two celebrated a one-year dating anniversary in February, but their relationship ended shortly thereafter. She insists they parted as friends. Levine continued as the bar manager until yesterday. Perhaps Mr. Levine simply didn't want to work for his ex-girlfriend, but this reporter wonders if there is more to the story."

"Anyone with information about the whereabouts of

Levine is asked to contact the Shady Grove Sheriff's Department," I finished. "That's it? What happened?"

"Check for a recent mention in the online database."

It only took a few minutes to search on the newer, much higher-performing machine. There wasn't a single article discussing a Miles Levine of the right age. We did find a lovely piece when Miles Levine of Ridgemont, Colorado retired after forty years as a high school football coach, but he wasn't the right age.

After going back to the *Sentinel's* database, I found the date of Hal Crews' follow-up article, two months after Miles disappeared. It was barely a sentence, hidden at the end of the Metro Section. Only the most dedicated newsreaders would have seen it.

"The investigation was closed," I told Walter. "Police found no signs of foul play. Since Levine was a grown man, they figured he left town."

"He moved away, changed his name, and was never heard from again?"

"There's a reason they call it 'living on the dl.'"

"No, they don't. Tell me no one says that."

I skimmed the page again. "No mention of where he went. Maybe the ghost scared him away. Leo died not long before his niece took over."

Digging through the stack of articles I'd printed, it only took a minute to find the obituary. In February 2001, Leo West suffered an unexpected fatal heart attack.

"Was he at the bar when he died? Maybe his spirit never left."

"It doesn't say. Just that he was survived by his sister, brother, and niece."

Walter jabbed his finger at the article, which made me

laugh because he went through the paper. "Look at those dates."

"What about them?"

"Leo West died in February 2001. In February 2002, his niece and Miles celebrated their one-year dating anniversary. Then Miles disappears. Maybe it's all related. What if Lucky killed her uncle to inherit the place, and Miles figured it out? There are plenty of ways to make something look like a heart attack."

My brow furrowed as I tried to follow his train of thought. "You don't think Leo's the ghost, do you? You think Lucky killed Miles, and he's haunting the bar?"

"It's one explanation for why he 'disappeared.'"

"All of his stuff was gone. Wouldn't they have found his car, at least?"

"She could have driven it into the Hudson River."

"Would she have reported him missing if she killed him?"

"What better way to throw suspicion off herself?" Walter said.

He had a point. We needed to question Lucky not only about Miles's disappearance and Leo's death, but whether she ever saw or heard anything supernatural while she was at the bar. We still didn't know exactly when the hauntings began—it wasn't easy to trace a rumor to the first time someone told it.

Going to the files yet again, I searched the *Sentinel* for the words "haunted" or "ghost" over the past hundred years. The first mention was in 2001.

"Look, Walter! Local resident reports hearing chains rattling when passing Two Mules late at night. The business was not open, and no other people were in sight." I smiled triumphantly. "There's our ghost."

"Who made the report?"

"It doesn't say. Why?"

"If I owned a haunted business, I wouldn't tell anyone," Walter said. "Just like you don't."

He had a point. "You think Leo started haunting the bar immediately after his death, but Lucky didn't tell anyone?"

"Exactly. Then she started bringing in workers. Leo tried to tell them what happened, but he scared them away instead."

"Maybe we've got it all backward. What if Leo's wife killed him, and he and Lucky happily hung out in the bar like us?"

"Add that to the list of things to ask Lucky. 'Was your ghost as cool as mine?'"

I snorted. "Let's keep looking."

An hour later, exactly one thing was clear: the answers we needed weren't in these microfilms. Everything else was muddled.

While rewinding the film on its spools and putting them away, I thought about what we knew. Normally, busywork helped me think. This time, no matter how I mulled it over, only one next step came to me.

"Let's go talk to Lucky," I said, stuffing all the printed articles into my bag.

Walter beamed. "I thought you'd never ask."

EIGHT

According to the Shady Grove Recorder of Deeds, Lucky Risk owned Two Mules from 2001 to 2004, which fit the date of Leo's death. There was no evidence of a house in Shady Grove County owned by her, but I lucked out when I found a single-family residence purchased by someone named George Risk back in 1972. It seemed likely that he was a relative, and the address was on my way home. Even if Lucky didn't live there, George might know where we could find her.

The Risk house was a cozy one-story, set in the middle of a decent-sized lot near the town's golf course. The blue-gray house had a pointed roof and a wooden door. Someone kept the lawn carefully maintained. A stone path led to a wooden porch with white railings. Flowerbeds beside the path contained some brownish plants that would probably lend additional charm to the property once spring rolled around.

Summoning my courage, I stepped onto the porch and knocked. A moment later, the door opened, and a white woman about my age, with brown hair pulled messily back peered out at me with sharp blue eyes surrounded by large, circular glasses. She wore high-end yoga pants similar to the ones I favored and wore several rings on each hand, plus large diamond earrings.

"Lucky?" I blurted, my surprise taking over for my manners.

In my head, anyone who was mature enough to own a bar in 2002 must have been one of those adulty adults, someone much wiser than me and obviously at least a decade older. At twenty-four, I'd been floating from one job to the next, trying to find my place: waitress, party planner, matchmaker. I'd been trying to find my calling, but nothing really fit. Lucky, apparently, was a more together twenty-something.

"Can I help you?" She gave me a pleasant but not overly friendly smile.

I introduced myself, then said, "I'm looking for Lucky Risk. I understand you used to own the bar down on Second Street."

She sighed heavily. "I'm sorry to say you've come to the right place. I'm Lucky. What's happened there now?"

"Nothing, why? Do you expect things to happen there?" She hesitated, and I continued, "A friend of mine is thinking about buying the property. I was hoping you could tell me about the history."

"History? Stay away, that's what I can tell you." She started to close the door.

Reaching out, I held it open. "Look, I know people think the bar is haunted. Rumor is, that's why you sold it. There's some weird energy there, and I'm wondering how much truth there is to the stories." She hesitated, and a plea entered my voice. "Please, I want to help my friend before someone gets hurt."

"You think it's haunted? What a laugh. The place is cursed." She sighed and opened the door further. "You better come in."

"Don't follow a stranger into their home!" Walter said. "It could be a trap!"

Quietly, I said, "I let you come as long as you promised not to cause trouble."

"What was that?" Lucky asked.

"Oh, I was just saying that you have a beautiful home." It wasn't a lie. The inside hallway was clean and well-lit, leading to a bright, open living room with a comfortable-looking blue couch and watercolors decorating the walls. "I love those paintings. Did you do them?"

"I did, thanks. Would you like some tea?"

"No, thanks, I'm fine." At her direction, I sat on one end of the couch. "Lucky. Is that a nickname?"

She snorted. "I wish. My mom used to say, with a last name like Risk, I needed some luck to balance me out. No one ever told her that not all luck is good, I guess. Lots of things happen to me by chance, that's for sure."

"You mean like never getting to open the bar? What happened?"

"Yeah, that was the worst luck of all."

Although she already knew why I was here, I took a deep breath before raising the subject again. "Rumor is, you sold the bar because it was haunted."

"Bah! The locals love getting caught up in all that lore; it brings the tourists in. When Nick started running tours a couple of years after I sold, I was so mad the thought never occurred to me. But that's got nothing to do with why we never opened after my uncle died. You know about Leo, right?" She took a long drink from her tea, as if trying to delay the conversation. "No, I got taken in by a smooth talker. Trusted the wrong person, and in the end, I lost everything."

I tried to meet Walter's eyes without her noticing. As far as I knew, Lucky was the only owner of this place. Did the person who took over in 2004 trick her into selling?

"It's a story as old as time," he said. "Get the details and make sure she doesn't leave out anything juicy."

"The newspaper said your bar manager ran away when you were preparing to reopen. That must've been rough."

She laughed bitterly. "You don't know the half of it."

"Let's start at the beginning," I said. "You inherited the bar in 2001, right? You would have been pretty young."

"I was finishing grad school when Uncle Leo died. You know, I didn't have any idea he planned to leave it to me. He was always my favorite adult relative. We'd hang out at all the family functions. Even waitressed at the bar over the summers during college." A soft sigh escaped her. "Aunt April said, when he made the will, they expected he'd show me the ropes before it belonged to me."

"She didn't want the bar?"

"Oh, no. The thing barely broke even. Leo always dreamed of running a bar, and he was great at pouring drinks, but he didn't have a head for business. That was one reason I wanted the degree. He invested April's salary over the years to keep it running, and I think that's a large part of why they divorced. When he passed, she was happy to be done with it."

"You weren't worried about taking on a failing business?"

"Oh, no! I had a bachelor's degree in business management, was months from getting my MBA, and was chock full of youthful optimism. I vowed to turn it around."

Not for the first time, I wondered what Ben was getting

himself into with this investment. It had been twenty years since anyone had operated a bar in Shady Grove, and apparently, it hadn't even made any money.

Ben was a grown man, though, and he was asking me for ghost expertise, not financial advice. Since he'd already accepted that he might buy a haunted business, the likelihood of not turning a profit seemed established.

"Had you always wanted to own a bar?"

"I always wanted to run a business, make my own decisions, and not have to answer to anyone." She laughed. "That was dumb. After the bar shut down, I got a job in the City. Worked fifteen years, retired early with plenty of money, and moved back here. None of it would have happened if that jerk hadn't left me."

"I'm glad everything turned around. What made you decide to sell the bar?"

"Miles did."

"You mean because he quit without notice?"

Lucky looked up, meeting my gaze for the first time since we'd started chatting. Setting her mug on the table, she leaned forward, hands on her knees. If I'd mimicked her pose, our knees would have touched.

"Oh, no. What he did was much worse than that. Listen, it's best to start at the beginning. We started dating shortly after Uncle Leo's funeral. It took a while for the place to go through probate, and Aunt April wasn't paying to keep the heat on—the pipes froze. Since the owner was dead, there was a whole mess with insurance. You don't want the details. Anyway, by the time I took possession of the bar and started the remodel, it had been closed at least six months. When we returned, everything was different. The place didn't feel the same."

"What happened?"

"Little things at first. The chandelier would sway like there was a breeze, but there weren't any windows open. Something thudding loudly on the roof. We tried to explain it away, like, 'Wow, that's a heavy squirrel' or 'Uncle Leo's saying hi!'"

My lips curved into a smile. "You had a friendly ghost."

"Hogwash," Walter said. "I can't do any of that stuff."

"Apparently, Uncle Leo didn't like it when Miles and I got serious. The weird things at the bar started getting worse, like stuff not being in the same place where we left it. It got bad. We were fighting all the time. Eventually, we broke up." She sighed. "He started seeing someone else right away. I was devastated, but he'd been such a help with the bar, I couldn't bring myself to fire him. I should have."

"Exes work together all the time," I said. "You couldn't have known he would take off."

"He didn't just run away. That's what the papers left out. He took the money for the bar's renovation with him."

I gasped. In the newspaper stories, the reporter made it sound like Miles was a nice guy who unexpectedly moved out of town. Now, he was a thief. Maybe the malevolent energy at the bar was Leo trying to avenge his niece, after all.

"You continued to work with Miles after he dumped you, and he stole everything?" I asked. "That's low. You couldn't open after that?"

"He took all the money. If the police had caught him, maybe it would have been okay, but no one ever saw him again. I couldn't pay my contractors. Believe it or not, I wound up finishing the roof repairs myself." A hollow laugh escaped her. "First storm of the year, it caved in. After that, I didn't have the heart to keep going. As much as giving up ate at my soul, I couldn't go back every day and face what happened. I applied for a job in the City, moved away, and tried not to look back. Took more than a decade before I even visited."

Before moving here, I would have naively asked "which city?" However, after only a few months in the area, I understood most people recognized New York City as the one "City." All others were lowercase. "I'm so sorry for what happened."

"Miles is probably living it up in Florida now, mooching off some other sad sack. I can't even find the poor woman to warn her." She shook her head. "Look at me, feeling sorry for myself. My life has been good since I left. Rumor says Uncle Leo's still haunting the bar. Maybe it never would have operated again, even if I'd stayed."

"Do you really believe that?"

"No. When the next owners lost the place, too, it was easy to say, 'See? What happened wasn't my fault. The bar's cursed.' But deep down, I knew. If Miles hadn't taken everything, we could have made it work. Even if Uncle Leo was hanging around, he didn't cause problems. Uncle Leo loved me; he wanted me to succeed. My problem was plain bad luck. The bar became an albatross around my neck. Even the upstairs apartment was terrible. It was drafty all the time. I brought in someone to look at the doors and windows, but he couldn't figure it out. Every time I approached the bookcases, I started shivering, like a ghost didn't want me to read."

This poor woman. All she wanted was to run her uncle's business and fall in love. Instead, her partner broke her heart, stole her money, and an angry ghost took over her business.

Twenty years ago, the Shady Grove police tried to find

Miles. By all accounts, they failed. I'd check the newspapers again and ask Tim what he knew about the investigation, but if Miles ever returned to town, Lucky would have heard about it. He was still out there, waiting to be brought to justice. The betrayal helped explain why the spirit at the bar didn't want anyone to enter. We needed to find Miles to make things right.

Unfortunately, he could be almost anywhere. I didn't have the investigative capabilities of even a two-person police force. Maybe I could perform a locator spell, but I'd have to go through the books to find one.

"Where was Miles from? Could he have returned to his hometown?"

She thought for a moment. "I'm sorry, I don't remember. A small town in Pennsylvania. It was close enough to go home for Thanksgiving, but too far for a regular weekend trip."

"You never went with him?"

"No. First, my family needed me. Then the bar needed both of us. Then he dumped me."

"Ask her about the cat," Walter prompted me. I blinked at him and waited for him to continue. "Where did the cat come from? Is it hers?"

Right. Well, it couldn't hurt to ask. "Did your uncle, by any chance, have a cat? Or did you?"

"No. Uncle Leo wanted a pet, but his wife was allergic. He was always feeding strays found near the bar. Drove Aunt April up the wall. Near the end of their marriage, he said he left out tuna so she wouldn't drop by."

"Your uncle sounds like quite a character," I said. "Can you think of anyone who might have wanted to harm him?"

She eyed me suspiciously. "Why?"

"You thought he was haunting the bar, but the being we

encountered wasn't friendly. The bar has a strange energy. I would call it malicious, if buildings could emote. My friend and I tried to go in, and something supernatural attacked us. It's hard to imagine why your uncle would hurt us unless he is trying to get revenge on Miles, and he's confused. Or unless someone killed him."

"Uncle Leo never liked Miles, so it's possible he wanted to warn me."

"I thought you started seeing each after Leo died?"

"Sure, but it's a small town. Miles's best friend worked on Second Street. They were always in the bar. He and Uncle Leo didn't get along. I should have asked if he had a good reason."

"You couldn't have known what would happen." Taking her hand between both of mine, I forced her to meet my gaze. "You are not cursed. Someone betrayed you, and I'm going to find him."

"It's sweet that you think so," she said. "At this point, I know better. Doesn't matter. It's all water under the bridge."

"We're done here," Walter said. "I feel bad for her, but she doesn't have anything else to give us."

Silently, I agreed with him; it was time to go. After reassuring Lucky once again that none of this was her fault, I grabbed my coat and headed for the door.

On the way out, I thought of one more thing. "This is going to sound weird, but do you have anything belonging to Miles? If we have some old clothes or something, I think we can find him."

"How?"

"Um, we can pull DNA from it," I lied. "If he ever used one of those find-a-family sites or got arrested, he might come up."

She scoffed. "Arrest is more likely. I hope you find him sitting in jail somewhere unpleasant. Ask him what he did with my money."

"I hope to do that," I said. "If you have anything, even an old t-shirt, it might be enough. Even if it's too late to get your money back, we might stop him from swindling anyone else."

She cleared her throat. "Help yourself. After he took off, I boxed up his stuff and put it in the basement under the bar. I'm pretty sure I didn't take it when I moved out. It's probably still there, along with the old tables and stuff."

"Why put Miles's stuff there?"

"I lived in the apartment overhead, so shoving it out of sight made sense. When I sold, I couldn't face going through everything. Sold the business as-is, everything included."

"You didn't want anything?"

"What am I going to do with a hundred-year-old cash register or twenty tables? Nah. Bad memories follow us all by themselves; there's no need to keep mementos."

It seemed unlikely that a box of clothes would still be in the basement after twenty years. One of the subsequent owners would have gone through the basement at some point and cleared it out.

"Who bought the bar?"

She shrugged. "My lawyer handled everything, and he moved to Florida years ago. I'd have to look for the records. You'll get them faster at Town Hall."

I thanked her and headed out. This visit gave me more information than expected: Leo was haunting the bar, he didn't like Miles, and Miles was the reason Lucky never reopened. Considering that Leo gave the business to Lucky, I understood why he was mad. We might need to bring

Miles in to resolve Leo's business, though, and I wasn't sure we could.

We weren't likely to find anything belonging to Miles in the basement. But it didn't matter whether the box was there, because we couldn't check. As long as a ghost blocked the entrance to the bar, I couldn't get anywhere near the basement.

CHAPTER
NINE

For Operation Bar Entry, Take Three, I called in the big guns. The ghost didn't want to talk to me. Since neither ghosts nor cats wore clothes, my thread magic was of limited use. The ghost also didn't want to talk to a fellow ghost, apparently. That left me with one option: see if he would talk to another cat.

When I explained my plan to Walter, he laughed. "Oh, I can't wait to watch this."

"It'll be fine," I said. "Pink is my familiar, right? He's supposed to help me."

"I'm sure he'll love to. It's getting him into the car that will be hilarious."

Since the idea of coaxing my cat into a vehicle already filled me with dread, I turned up the radio and ignored Walter.

Convincing Pink to visit the bar with me turned into quite an event. And by "quite an event," I meant "an epic disaster." Like the time I tried to make a soufflé.

When I was a kid, Grandma Vera lured her cat into the carrier for vet trips using a multi-step process. Step one, set the carrier in the main living space, two to three days before the intended car trip. Step two, ignore it. Step three, open the door at least a day before the visit. Step four, ignore again, and hope the cat forgot. Step five, lead a trail of cat treats to the carrier, put cat nip inside, and wait.

The initial problem with this plan was that I preferred not to wait almost a week before returning to the bar. The second problem was that Walter didn't own a cat carrier. When I asked him about it, he laughed. The third was that my cat almost certainly wouldn't get into such a thing of his own volition. Unfortunately, for Pink's safety, he needed a carrier. When I asked Walter if he had one, he just snorted.

Deciding to tackle the second problem first, before going home, I stopped and bought the most luxurious, dignified cat carrier available. It was made of fabric, unlike the hard plastic cases I'd seen as a kid. The soft mesh sides gave the occupant a full 360° view of the world around them. The bottom was lined with the softest wool I'd ever touched.

Back home, I abbreviated Grandma Vera's approach. Leaving the carrier on the floor in the foyer, I opened the door and sprinkled catnip inside.

"You don't think Pink is that stupid, do you?" Walter appeared at my elbow. "I'm more likely to get into that thing than he is."

"Now that I would pay to see."

"Your grandfather is right." Pink jumped on top of the carrier, then sat and looked at me with his unnerving directness. "I am not your pet, and I won't allow you to carry me around like a common companion. What is the meaning of this indignity?"

"Don't think of it as an insult. Think of it as this is your chariot, O Emperor, and I am but a servant transporting you where you wish to go."

"Nice try. Out of curiosity, where do you think I wish to go?"

"To Two Mules," I said. "Ben and I discovered something I'd like you to see."

"Did you take a photograph?" he asked.

"I tried to take video, but it didn't work. We'd like you to talk to the ghost for us."

Walter rubbed his hands together. "Oh, this will be great! Can I come?"

"You were already there once, and you ran," I pointed out.

"I wasn't prepared. It was scary. You didn't tell me the bar was scary."

Pink moved his gaze to my grandfather. "You're a ghost. What could you possibly be afraid of?"

"This ghost moves things! All I do is wave my arms and yell. No one ever hears me. But a big wind kicks up when you approach this bar, and there's a big scary cat."

"You're taking me talk to a cat?" Pink raised an eyebrow. "Why don't you call animal control? Or bring the cat here."

"Because it's dead," I said. "It's a ghost."

"You're the ghost whisperer, not me."

I sighed. "Please?"

"You know I'm intrigued by this whole situation. I'm happy to talk to the ghostly cat if you can get him here. I'm not riding in the car. Terrible means of travel. Extremely unsafe."

"Car safety has come a long way since Walter was alive. You'll be fine."

"Yes, I will, because I'm staying here."

Pleadingly, I turned to my grandfather. "Can you help?"

He snorted. "I had to pay the vet to come here for years. What's the deal, Pink?"

"None of your business," he said.

"Did I mention the ghost is a cat?"

"More than once. Fascinating, really."

"Great! Get in the car."

Pink snorted. "Nope."

For a long moment, I glared at my cat, cursing myself for not expecting this turn of events. Most cats objected to carriers, but if he agreed to sit in his seat, I wasn't terribly worried about letting him wander. Unfortunately, there was no way I could carry Pink to the car over his objection without the carrier.

Unless I could magic it into a giant saucer of milk, Pink would never climb into the tiny cage.

Hmmm...

Although the flexible sides had interior support, the outer covering was cloth. Thread sewed the panels together. Both things gave me an advantage. With a deep breath, I reached for my magic. Once I had it firmly in hand, I let out a sigh. "Fine. You win."

Pink licked his front left paw. While he focused on his bath, I sent magic into every thread of the carrier and asked it to release.

The top of the carrier fell. Pink's eyes flew open. I asked the fabric panels to reform around my cat and sew themselves together. He bolted.

Now I had carrier pieces with no stitches and no cat. With a flick of my wrist, I sent the panels after him.

Pink raced into the dining room. The carrier followed, with me half a step behind. Walter's laughter echoed behind us.

Inside the dining room, Pink bolted under a table. The

carrier zoomed after him, sending a chair toppling. Pink jumped on top of the table. When I sent the carrier at him again, he swatted the panels away.

Helplessly, I watched Pink and the panels move from one spot to the next, trying desperately to figure out my next move.

Pink needed to come with me. Coming with me required a cat carrier. I had to win this battle. As futile as this effort appeared, I'd committed myself and I needed—

"STOP!" The booming voice filled the space, reverberating off the walls. "THAT IS ENOUGH!"

I froze. The carrier pieces dropped to the ground.

Josie stood in the kitchen door, arms crossed over her chest. If this were a cartoon, smoke would be pouring out of her ears. "What on earth is going on?"

"Emma thought she'd like to embarrass herself," Pink said.

My cheeks flamed. "I, um, need to take Pink in the car. He doesn't want to go."

"And you think that you, a fledgling hedge witch, can best a magical cat?"

At her words, Pink sat up straight as if preening.

I stuck my tongue out at him. "Not so much beat as out think."

It still sounded stupid.

Josie's head shake confirmed as much. "Sort it out. I'm cooking in here, and I can't focus with all this racket. You'll bring half the neighborhood to see what is going on."

"I should be allowed to do magic in my own house," I grumbled.

"Then do it quietly," she retorted.

Her tone made it clear this conversation was over. I might be the boss here, but I didn't dare antagonize Josie when she was this angry. Not least of which because she was cooking dinner, and her emotions tended to wind up in the food.

"I'm sorry, Josie." With a flick of my wrist, the cat carrier returned to its original state. On the floor, closed, empty of cats.

"That's better," she said. "Now, Pink, what do you have to say for yourself?"

"She was trying to put me in a cage. I am the wronged party."

"You couldn't have removed yourself from the situation? Don't you teleport?"

He averted his eyes and sneezed, as if he couldn't bear to agree with her.

"Hold up," I said. "Can you teleport to the bar?"

"It's too far," he grumbled.

Josie put her hands on her hips. "There must be a reasonable compromise. Pink, why don't you want to go in the car?"

"I don't trust them," he grumbled.

"You'd be safe in the carrier," I pointed out.

"That's a non-starter. But I will go in the car if you put feeders outside the ballroom windows so I can watch the birds."

By now, I would have agreed to almost anything. "Fine. I'll buy one."

"Ten."

Good thing we had a lot of land here.

"Done," I said. "As long as you don't bring me any 'presents.'"

He snorted derisively.

"Anything else, Your Highness?" I asked.

Josie said my name in that mom tone of hers, warning me not to antagonize the creature whose help I needed.

Finally, Pink said, "I want to know I'm appreciated."

"As much as I do *not* appreciate what just happened," I said. "I love you and am extremely grateful for all you do."

"Fine. Let's go."

"My plan would have worked on a regular cat," I huffed.

"Let this be a reminder to you," Josie said. "Never underestimate your familiar."

"Yes, ma'am. Pink, are you ready?"

"Can I drive?"

A snort escaped me. "Don't push it. If you don't give me any more trouble, I *might* let you pick the music."

"Deal."

Ben met us in the driveway as I was opening the door to let Pink into the front passenger seat. I glanced from him to the cat. "Uh, I think you'll have to sit in the back."

"What do you mean, 'think'?" Pink asked.

Ben laughed and opened the rear door.

"Did you understand him?" I asked.

"The look on his face didn't require an interpreter."

"Are we going to leave, or are you two going to chat all day?" Pink asked.

Trying not to roll my eyes, I slid into my seat and pushed the start button. Minutes later, we were on our way.

Once again, when we arrived on Second Street, I scanned for a parking space while still blocks away from Two Mules. We needed every possible advantage, and the element of surprise couldn't hurt.

Unless, of course, the spirit hated surprises.

"Park here," Pink ordered. "I don't want the ghost to see us together."

I gave him the side-eye as I maneuvered into a parking spot by the coffee shop. If he didn't mind the walk, neither did I. "You, a cat, are worried about being seen with me, a human?"

"That's what I said, isn't it?"

"I know we don't know each other well, but that hurts," Ben said.

"The last time you were here, you got attacked." He studied me for a minute. "Are you sure you don't want me to turn you into a cat?"

My mouth dropped open. "You can do that?"

"I won't know unless I try. I'm sure I could undo it if necessary."

"Thanks, but no." Last year, a friend of a friend got stuck in bunny form after shifting—a trick he'd done hundreds of times. It took five of us to undo the spell keeping him trapped, so I'd rather not take my chances. Having two legs was fine with me.

"If you're sure." Pink's tone sounded like I told him lima beans tasted better than chocolate ice cream.

"What's the plan?" I asked while parking on the street.

"I am the plan."

Ben made a noise that sounded suspiciously like he was trying to smother a laugh.

"Okay, sure. What are you going to do?"

"You'll see."

"May I make a suggestion before you go up against a potentially violent ghost by yourself?"

Pink eyed me warily. "If you must."

"If you wear a bandana or something, you can send me a message if you need me. I know you've got everything under control, but nothing is for certain. We aren't even positive what we're dealing with."

He arched an eyebrow. "That thing in there isn't sure what *it* is dealing with."

It took every ounce of restraint I possessed not to roll my eyes. Instead, I pushed a button with emphasis, unlocking the doors. "Fine. Go. Do your thing. Awe us peons with your amazingness. I'll take a nap since you don't need me."

"You're going to make me ask you to open the doors, aren't you? Need I point out that I have no interest in this bar and I'm only here as a favor to you?"

"Em, it's probably not a great idea to antagonize our last hope," Ben said.

"Your friend is wise," my cat agreed. "Now let me out."

Without meeting his eyes, I pushed the button to roll down the passenger window. He peered out, looking down and up before stepping cautiously onto the door frame. Instead of jumping down as expected, he turned and hopped onto the top of the car with a thud.

It reverberated through the car.

"He wants to be very clear about who owns whom, doesn't he?" Ben asked.

"Oh, yeah."

Then Pink pushed his point further by sauntering down the windshield. He paused on the hood to lick his back paw before hopping to the ground.

Despite my indignation at the suggestion that he couldn't be seen with the likes of us, letting Pink go in first made sense. If the ghost were only opposed to humans, he could get a feel for the place without our interference.

Before exiting my car, I counted to one hundred. Pink had nearly made it to the bar by the time I finished. Ben followed a few paces behind.

Trying to look casual, I climbed onto the wooden sidewalk and examined the coffee shop's window. Thunder rumbled in the distance. Hopefully, the storm held off, because Pink would race back to the car at the first raindrop. I continued to the next storefront, scrutinizing every detail like someone would quiz me later.

When we were about fifty feet from the bar, Pink meowed loudly. The thunder rumbled again.

No, wait. That wasn't thunder. It was a growl, exactly like the one before I got attacked. A chill went down my spine. Pink said he would be fine, but I'd grown attached to the little fuzzball.

My first instinct was to run in and scoop him up, but my legs wouldn't move. Whether fear or a spell, I didn't know. All I could do was watch and pray I hadn't made a huge mistake.

Ben put a hand on my arm, as if to warn me not to interfere. The gesture comforted me, both as a reminder that Pink could handle himself and that I wasn't alone. We were in this together.

Undeterred by the warning growls, Pink looked up at the building and meowed again. A white and caramel figure passed through the door. He slid through the air like butter, moving with the grace of, well, a cat.

The beast studied Pink for about half a second before lunging. Part of me expected him to go right through my pet, despite what happened to me and Walter. What I didn't expect was for my cat to disappear and materialize a foot away.

When Josie mentioned teleporting, I thought it was hyperbole. Once my shock passed, it explained a lot.

Beside me, Ben asked, "Did he just...?"

"Yup."

The ghost lunged again. This time, Pink opened his

mouth. The sound that came out was somewhere between a screech and a howl. It echoed down the street, rolling past me with such power, the windows vibrated.

The ghost dropped like he'd hit a brick wall. He fell to the ground, unmoving.

"This is so weird," Ben said.

"What happened? Did my cat drop a ghost? Can he do that with human ghosts?"

"I would give anything to answer those questions. Instead, I feel an overwhelming urge to go to church," Ben said.

Watching my cat take on a ghost in an epic magic battle made me feel even more ridiculous about trying to defeat him myself. He was going to get a truckload of treats as an apology. After erecting the bird feeders, I might have to fill the pool with cat nip.

I stepped toward them, but Pink turned and met my eyes. He shook his head before turning back to his nemesis.

Pink reared back on his hind feet. He and the ghost engaged in a "conversation" of mewls, hisses, and growls that were completely incomprehensible. My mentor told me once I was one of the very few humans who understood Pink most of the time. Apparently, my cat wanted privacy.

After they spoke, the ghost lowered his head to the sidewalk. He rubbed his cheek against the ground before flopping down. After a moment, he rolled over, exposing his belly.

Pink stepped forward and sniffed the ghost before giving a tentative lick. He meowed one last time at the ghost before trotting back toward us.

"You're welcome," he said.

I glanced toward the ghost, but the three of us now stood alone in the street.

"Whoa," Ben said.

"My sentiments exactly," I said. "That was intense. Are you okay?"

"Yeah. Stunned, but okay," he said. "Did your cat remove a malevolent spirit from the bar?"

"I have no idea."

"Did you doubt me?" Pink asked. "What are you waiting for? Go inside. I'll wait out here."

"Not to, uh, question you, sir," Ben said to Pink, "but are you sure it's safe for us?"

"Of course it is. Don't be ridiculous."

"What happened?" I asked.

"I met GhostCat," Pink said.

"A ghost cat? Yeah, I know."

"Not 'A ghost cat.' GhostCat. That's his name. Fitting, isn't it? GhostCat lives at the bar with another spirit. He is fiercely protective and quite loyal. Wouldn't tell me anything about his companion. No name, age, gender, nothing. But I convinced him we mean no harm. I explained you want to use the space for humans, and no one will bother them. Most people won't see him if he doesn't want them to. Being visible to the living takes energy."

"And he was okay with that?" I was so bewildered at what I'd witnessed that my brain was only picking up about half of Pink's words, like it was operating at half speed.

"He doesn't care how the living make money. I explained that you have a calling to help ghosts resolve their unfinished business. His companion has that, which is why they remain in the bar. He's willing to give you a chance."

"Will the master talk to me? What's his or her name?"

"I didn't get the companion's name, but GhostCat agreed to let you inside for further evaluation."

"How?" Ben asked.

"Easy. My power is stronger than his. He doesn't want to cross me. If you cause problems, he might change his mind."

"What problems could I cause a ghost?" I asked.

"Exorcism?" Pink said sardonically. "Tread carefully. If either of them decides they don't trust your motives, GhostCat will make what happened during your first visit look like a love tap. But you should be fine for now."

The words reverberated through the air. *For now.* At the moment, Pink could overpower GhostCat, which scared the spirit. *For now.* We were safe. *For now.*

What would happen to me and Ben if GhostCat's power grew beyond Pink's while we were inside the building?

TEN

Although GhostCat's parting comment to Pink sounded ominous, there was no option other than for me and Ben to press forward. That was why we were here. If anything went wrong, Pink would still be nearby. Overall, we should be safe.

Before we crossed the threshold, Pink returned to the car to rest, claiming he was "too bored" to continue helping us. I guessed the interaction with GhostCat wore him out more than he wanted to admit, so I didn't argue. Ben must've shared my assessment, because he promised to get some milk from the coffee place before we went home.

After all the effort of getting access to this building, I almost expected the sky to open and angels to sing when Ben removed the caution tape and we finally walked through the doors. Alas, nothing so exciting happened.

Ben and I found ourselves in a dark, dusty room that must have once been beautiful. With the windows boarded up, we couldn't see much beyond the light spilling in the open doorway.

The red velvet fabric on the walls must have once been

thick and luxurious; now the panels were faded and full of moth holes. Poor things. I reached out with my magic to pet the walls, thanking the threads for hanging in there all this time and letting them know we planned to restore them. Instantly, they brightened. If Ben weren't here, I'd bring them back to their full glory.

A wooden bar ran along the far wall, nothing but dust on the surface. The dirt-streaked mirror hanging behind it revealed me, Ben, and a massive empty room. Sawdust coated the floor, even after all this time.

"Do you see a light switch?" I asked.

"Wouldn't matter," Ben said. "The gas and electric have been off for years. It's not mine yet, and the ghost never paid the bill."

I forced a laugh, although I wasn't sure he was kidding. A glance at his expression told me he didn't know, either.

Using my phone's flashlight, I walked around, checking each wall and peering into corners. What I hoped to find was anyone's guess, since spirits didn't leave calling cards. Maybe I expected GhostCat to come out, but he was nowhere to be found.

Finally, I simply called out, "Hello? Anyone there? I'm here to help."

A loud creaking was my only response. Ben and I looked at each other. I pushed on the floor beneath my feet and listened. Nothing. Ben did the same. Then a second creaking. Something crashed. I jumped. Ben yelled. A third person screamed.

In the distance, a door slammed.

The hair on my arms stood up.

What was going on?

"It's not a ghost," I said, trying to sound certain. "Ghost can't slam doors."

"Ghosts can't hit you, either, but one did. I can't hear ghosts, and I heard that."

"Touché."

"Hello?" he called. "Anyone up there?"

No response.

"Do you hear anything?" he asked after a moment.

"I don't," I whispered. "Maybe it's a manifest spirit?"

"What's the difference?"

"Manifest spirits can, apparently, rattle chains and slam doors." I took a deep breath to calm myself. Raising my voice, I yelled, "Leo, is that you? Don't be afraid."

The chandelier above our heads began swinging. An icy wind filled the space.

I shivered. "What's going on?"

"I'm no expert, but I'd say 'there's something strange in your neighborhood.'" The words were light, but my friend still looked uneasy.

For Ben's sake, I forced a smile. "Who you gonna call?"

Before he could respond, the lights in the chandelier flickered. Our spirit apparently wasn't a *Ghostbusters* fan.

"Um, isn't the electricity off?"

"Yes, it is," Ben said. "I thought you said the ghost was okay with us?"

"GhostCat said we could enter," I said. "But he's not the only one here. Apparently, his companion wants to say hello." I lifted my gaze to the ceiling. "Are you hurt? Who killed you?"

The lights in the chandelier blazed before fading out, leaving us again in near darkness. Spots danced before my eyes.

Ben came over and put his hand on my arm. "Are you okay?"

"I think so," I said, giving him a big hug. We both

needed it. "This is way beyond my realm. I need to do a lot of research on unfriendly spirits. Did you feel a rush of wind? Hear the screams?"

"All of it. I never wanted to believe the rumors, but I don't know what else to think."

A shadow fell across the doorway, taking most of our light. "Hello? Is anyone there?"

Ghosts didn't block light or create shadows, so this had to be a real person coming to see what was going on.

Before I could decide how to proceed, Ben stepped forward. "Good morning! Ben Cartwright. This is my associate, Emma."

Shining my flashlight at our visitor helped me get vague impressions of a guy who appeared to be in his early-twenties. He had close-cropped hair almost as red as mine, a neatly trimmed goatee, too much self-tanning lotion, and a shady look about him.

The guy grinned broadly as he waltzed into the room. His attitude made me want to ask GhostCat to shove him outside, but at least we could see a little better. "TJ Crews. I work for the *Shady Grove Sentinel*."

"Crews? Any relation to Hal?"

"You know my dad?!"

"No, actually. I was looking through old newspaper articles, and his name popped up a lot."

"Yeah, Dad moved to editor. Now I'm the reporter," he said. "Are you moving in? I thought the town owned this place."

"They do," Ben said. "Emma and I are looking around."

"Say, you haven't seen or heard anything suspicious, have you?" He lowered his voice. "Rumor has it this place is haunted."

Ben grunted. "Yeah, I've heard. At first I thought

someone was trying to drive the customers elsewhere, avoid healthy competition. But there's nowhere else to go."

"Oh, it's more than that. Listen, could I interview you for the paper? We could do a whole feature about how you refuse to be scared away. You're not a linebacker, are you? That would really give some heft to the story."

I stifled a laugh. Ben was in good shape, but he looked more like a long-distance runner than a football player.

"Sorry, no," Ben said.

TJ turned to me. "What about you? Any karate in your background?"

"I'm a friend," I said firmly. "No story here."

"Why do you look so familiar?" He narrowed his eyes as if unsure whether to believe me, but I smiled serenely at him. After a minute, he offered a business card to Ben. "If you change your mind, call me. I'd love to run an exclusive about the new bar. It'll be great publicity for you."

Ben pocketed the card. "Thanks."

Together, we moved into the doorway, giving TJ little choice but to step out onto the sidewalk. We followed, watching him turn toward Town Square.

"I don't trust that guy," Ben finally said.

"He makes my skin itch."

"That's because he's as shady as this grove!" A voice rang out from the right.

I jumped. When I turned, a burly white man with a bushy gray beard and wire-rimmed sunglasses stood doubled over, laughing at his own joke. Finally, he straightened up and held out his right hand. "Floyd Fisher. I own the place next door. Bait and Switch."

We exchanged a look. Surely the man who worked next to the bar knew a thing or two about its history. As Ben introduced us, a jingling bell drew our attention to the store on the other side.

Floyd spotted the newcomer first, yelling over my shoulder, "Grace! What are you doing? Did you come to harass these honest folks? I told you to leave them alone!"

The woman who stepped out the door of the adjacent building had ombre blond hair, a golden tan *much* more natural-looking than TJ's, and sharp features. I estimated her to be around my age. She wore a pink apron over a pink and white t-shirt and soft-looking gray pants. My powers told me they were sweatpants material, made to look like slacks. Brilliant.

She smiled at me and Ben before sneering at Floyd. "I came to warn them about the local riff-raff, but it looks like I'm too late. That guy in the tackle shop? He's the worst. Used to drive my father up the wall before he retired."

Oh, Bait and Switch. I smiled at the newcomer. "Tackle? That explains the name."

"You'd think so, but what you see inside isn't what you'd expect." Floyd winked at me.

"What brings you folks here to our little strip of side-walk?" Grace asked. "Normally, this is cordoned off for safety."

"I bet TJ took the tape down!" Floyd declared.

"Actually, no, that was us," Ben said. "I'm thinking about moving in."

"Oh, what a marvelous idea!" Grace beamed. "It's been empty for so long; people talk. You'll breathe some new life into the strip."

"That's what I think," Ben said.

"My name's Grace, as Floyd said. I own the candy shop next door, Cocoa Channel. Like Coco Chanel, get it? I came over because I heard someone scream. Is everything okay?"

"We're fine," I said. "Um, that was me. It's really dark in there, and then TJ appeared in the doorway a bit abruptly. I overreacted."

"The rumors have us a little on edge," Ben said. "I'm sure you've heard them?"

"Of course we have," Floyd said. "You don't need to worry, though. Grace's personality is enough to scare most ghosts away."

"That's your BO," she shot back.

"Being on both sides, you two are in the perfect position to see everything. Do you know what's going on?" I asked.

Floyd chortled. "Oh, this is great! You think it's haunted? Sure thing, Kiddo. Why don't we do a ghost hunt and then you can pay me fifty bucks to read your fortune."

"Your fortune is: you will soon be fifty dollars poorer," Grace warned. "Don't listen to him. Floyd doesn't believe in any of that."

"Do you?"

"Unexplainable things happen over there. Maybe it's a ghost, maybe it's not, but I'm no fool. Back when the rumors first started, people brought in that TV show, *Ghost Hunters*. It was brilliant! They found ectoplasmic activity, got some recordings, and everything. That's all the proof I need to stay on this side of the walls. That's when I put the police tape up. It's a constant reminder."

"They were con artists," Floyd said. "Their recording was radio static with some feedback thrown in. Any truck driver could replicate it."

"Anyway," Grace said loudly, "it was great fun for a while. After Nick bought the place, he did ghost tours."

"Disgusting opportunist." Floyd spat on the floor, then flushed. "Sorry."

Grace continued as if he hadn't said anything. "He

bought around 2010, maybe? It might have been earlier, but definitely after the roof caved in. Doesn't matter. Theatrical guy, young at the time. He saw a rerun of *Ghost Hunters* and wanted to profit from it. Advertised, bought a bunch of ridiculous costumes, and played up the rumors."

"How did that go over?" I asked. "Was he selling drinks?"

"Oh, no. Just the tours. Nick did decent business at first, but the mayor didn't like the negative publicity. She passed a resolution that shut him down, so he listed the bar. No one would touch a haunted property—who wants a business they can't operate? Then he tried to claim it wasn't haunted, and there was a big lawsuit. Made the national papers and everything."

"They made me do a deposition," Floyd grunted. "Never felt so foolish."

"What happened?" I asked.

"The judge said, after running ghost tours and profiting from claiming a ghost lived at Two Mules, he couldn't change his mind when it was time to sell. Nick advertised it as haunted, and he made money, therefore, as far as the law was concerned, this building is haunted. The bar is one of the few legally haunted properties in the United States." Grace beamed with pride.

Whatever puts you on the map.

"That's a great story for the tourists," Ben said, "but no one believes in ghosts, do they? I figured the prior owners had a run of bad luck."

"Everyone has a story about strange things happening around here," Floyd said. "There are too many tales for all of them to be true. You'd need a dozen ghosts to do that much haunting. The stories have taken on a life of their own."

"What do you think?" I asked Grace.

Grace shivered and made the sign of the cross. "I'm no expert, but between the TV show and the ghost tours, you couldn't pay me to go in there."

These two certainly made an interesting pair of neighbors. Although they must be about twenty years apart in age, they had the easy rapport that comes with knowing someone for decades.

"Being right next door, you must have known Lucky," I said, trying to ease the conversation in the right direction. Okay, subtlety wasn't my strong suit.

Grace waved one hand. "Oh, we go way back. All the way to kindergarten. Shady Grove's a small place. She was a year ahead of me, but in a school with a hundred kids, you know everyone."

"Were you friends?"

"I wouldn't say that. She dated my best friend for a while." She sighed and shook her head. "I still can't believe how that played out."

"Miles? When he disappeared, it must have come as quite a shock," I said.

"I never suspected a thing. He didn't breathe a word."

"You want to know about Miles?" Floyd asked. "What a mess. Grace here was devastated when he ran away."

"Well, I'm stronger now, at least. Better off without him, even if old Floyd is the only person I have to talk to most of the time," Grace said.

"Do either of you own a cat?" Ben asked. "We thought we saw one lurking around here the other day."

"A cat? Don't say that too loudly. The tourists will come rushing back if they think we've got a ghost *and* a cat," Floyd said.

"That's enough ghost talk." Grace looked queasy. "Did

you know these three buildings used to be one? Oh, it was magnificent."

"Really? Was it one enormous bar?"

She shook her head. "Carl's Carriage Emporium. My great-great-grandfather opened the business before everyone had cars. Carriages were big, you know, took up a lot of space. He sold all the accouterments, too. Blankets, covers, spare parts, and wheels, plus horse feed and supplies."

Looking around, I tried to envision what she was saying. "I wish I could have seen it. It sounds beautiful."

"Me, too." She sighed. "It closed before I was born. A place like that couldn't exist now, but candy is nice, too. Come on, Floyd, we've taken up enough of these people's time."

"You don't need to ask me twice," Floyd said. "This place creeps me out."

After they left, Ben and I went back inside. Ben started taking pictures and measurements of the space, tapping notes into his phone, and muttering to himself. He wanted to bring in a structural engineer to inspect the building as soon as possible now that we had access.

While he worked, I explored. There had been no sign of GhostCat since our arrival, and I hoped to find him with his master. Assuming the master had originally been human, we had a lot to talk about.

I poked into a few corners, even peeked in the oven, before realizing how ridiculous this was. Where did a ghost hide? They didn't. Most people couldn't see them.

"I'm going to check upstairs," I called to Ben.

"Be careful!" he called back. "They were built over a hundred years ago, and I haven't had anyone check the structural integrity yet."

Although the building was old, it seemed in good shape. Maybe it helped that the owners of the adjacent buildings kept things up, or the ghost had been a contractor during their lifetime. Either way, I didn't notice any holes in the walls, water stains, or other major issues. Everything looked pretty good, and the stairs didn't even creak beneath my weight.

The apartment covered the entire upstairs floor space, making it much bigger than any place I'd ever rented. Massive windows brought in natural light and gave a view of Town Hall in the distance. One bedroom took up the entire back wall, with windows overlooking a small parking lot. The drafty bookcases Lucky mentioned lined one wall, a once-beautiful carved mahogany covered in a thick layer of dust.

The only other thing in the room was a hideous, burnt orange shag carpet from the 1970s in the middle of the living room floor. I strongly supported the prior occupant's decision to leave it behind.

I poked around the upstairs as best I could with only my phone's flashlight. We'd have to bring a lantern next time, unless I took the boards off the windows.

Back downstairs, the first door I peered into was a storage room. There was another door on the far wall. It didn't look like it faced the parking lot, but I checked it, anyway. About a foot from the door, I stopped.

GhostCat lay on the floor, watching me. This close, I noted that one of his eyes was green, the other yellow.

"Good morning," I murmured. "Thank you for allowing us in. That was an impressive light show earlier."

He watched me, not moving a muscle.

"How did you do it?"

No answer, obviously.

"Is your master around?"

Again, nothing but that unnerving stare. I wasn't terribly surprised. Although Walter lived in my ballroom and roamed the house at will, it took energy to make himself seen. After almost thirty years alone, he had a lot stored up. But if he got tired or didn't want to talk to anyone, he vanished in the blink of an eye.

For all I knew, Leo's ghost was in this room, standing beside the cat, laughing at me. If he possessed enough energy to have not only a ghostly familiar but one who could attack people, Leo was far stronger than anything I'd ever encountered. Until he could be persuaded to show himself, I had no idea how to convince him to move on.

ELEVEN

After leaving the bar, I swung by the mansion to drop off my companions and eat lunch before taking Walter back to the library. He might not be able to pull microfilm, but he could read printed pages, and his insights were spot-on. It was nice to have someone to bounce ideas off, even if I had to put in my earbuds to pretend I was on the phone.

When we arrived, the boxes of microfilm sat exactly where we'd left them in the "Return for Filing" bin, untouched. I scooped them up, found the date I wanted, and loaded the film in minutes.

"We're getting good at this," I joked. "Time for a career change?"

"Helping ghosts is your career change," Walter replied.

Part of me wondered if Leo's ex-wife caused his death, so we started by going back to their original marriage announcement in the early 1980s. Then I searched for her name, too. The database returned very little information about her. She was in her fifties when the couple divorced.

Only one article came up after that: her obituary, dated seven years ago.

"Maybe she's the ghost," Walter said.

"Only if they've got a full-on party going." I pointed at the dates. "The sightings predate her death by about a dozen years."

"What about deaths in general?" Walter said. "Can you search for all murders? There can't have been many in such a small town. This ain't Cabot Cove."

"All deaths since 2001?"

"All deaths period."

"You think the ghost was long dead before the first sighting? How could that be?"

"Who has more experience as a ghost, you or me?" he retorted. "We don't always make ourselves known. Maybe the construction disturbed them. Or they got upset by Leo and his wife bickering. The ghost might have wanted revenge for having their peaceful rest interrupted."

The theory seemed unlikely to me, but I humored him.

Searching turned out to be fruitless. Lots of people died in the days before modern medicine. It was nearly impossible to distinguish suspicious deaths. The obituaries didn't include photographs. The information must be out there somewhere, but I didn't know how to find it in the near future.

"Maybe the librarian has an idea," I said. "I'll ask her."

When we approached the reference desk, Consuela jumped to her feet with a huge smile. "Emma! I didn't know you were coming back!"

"She looks ecstatic to see you. How much did you donate?"

"I wasn't sure I'd be in," I said. "We—I mean, I—didn't want to bother you again."

"Bother?" She snorted. "If I'd been expecting you, I'd have thrown a parade. Not nearly enough people are interested in the area's history or improving the library. Girl, you're my new best friend if you'll have me."

"So a lot then," Walter said.

Her praise made me a little uncomfortable. I was glad no one but my grandfather was around to hear. Clearing my throat, I said, "We should get lunch sometime. For now, how far back do the *Sentinel* articles go?"

She looked positively giddy. "If you're interested in history, I could get you the very first issue. January 25, 1693."

"I'm very impressed that you know that."

She beamed. "Established as soon as the town got up and running. The founders escaped Salem, Massachusetts during the witch trials, and they wanted the world to know what was happening."

Her impressive grasp of history made me wonder if it might be possible to avoid digging through the articles again. "Did you ever hear anything about anyone dying under suspicious circumstances?"

"Back then? Hard to say. There were so many people passing through in those days because we're near the Hudson River. I'm sure there were accidents, but I can't think of any big events."

"This area used to be busy?" I tried to keep the incredulity out of my voice.

"Oh, yes! With the top of the Hudson nearby, we were an important stop on the way to Canada. People came from miles away to view the cascading water. It's how our town got its name."

"If she tells you a girl named Willow fell in the water, get out of here," Walter said.

I smothered a snort-laugh. "I've never seen the falls, but I hear they're beautiful. I didn't realize they were part of the Hudson."

"Oh, yes. This area provided key support to the logging industry back in the day." She shook her head and checked her watch. "Listen to me. I'd love to help, but it's time for story hour. The regular reader is out sick, so I'm filling in. If you're here when we're done, let's chat."

"I'm going with her," Walter said. "They're doing *Library Lion* today, and it looks good."

I gazed at him. "How do you know?"

"Watching you scroll is boring. I'm insulted you didn't even see me slip away. I'll be back."

"Go ahead. I'm going to read about Nick's haunted bar tours."

This search turned up a wealth of information. Not only did my man Hal Crews post a rave review of the tours' opening, but Nick advertised at least once a week. The past issues gave a clear timeline from when he sold the first tickets until the eventual closing and ill-fated sale.

After that, there was no mention of the bar in the papers other than a note that the Supreme Court of the United States had declined to review the case. I never found mention of an owner after Nick. It looked like he'd stopped paying the property taxes and moved away. A couple of years later, the town foreclosed. Since then, the place had sat empty, waiting for someone to come along and exorcise the ghosts.

I'd love to talk to Nick, but the foreclosure notice was the last time his name appeared in the *Shady Grove Sentinel*.

The library's database included major state and national papers, not only the tiny local ones. I checked Saratoga, Albany, Boston, and even the *New York Times*, but nothing said what happened to the prior owner. I even found a New Orleans newspaper to see if he'd moved his ghost tour business, but if so, he'd changed his name. The man might as well have been a ghost himself.

TWELVE

After leaving the library, I didn't have any more clarity than before. We knew Leo was the last person who owned the bar before the ghost rumors started. Lucky took over. She and Miles were getting serious before he abruptly broke it off. Then Miles stole all Lucky's money and ran away. What happened next? How did it all tie together?

Leo had died of a heart attack, hadn't he? Considering the lack of other potential ghostly suspects, I wondered. If only he'd appear, we could ask.

Unfortunately, the only spirit to show themselves was GhostCat. He either didn't speak English, or didn't want to speak to me. I could bring in Pink to get more information, but I preferred a lighter touch. There had to be a second spirit here.

In all the lore about Two Mules, no one mentioned a cat. The newspaper articles provided reports of *humans* moaning, rattling chains, and other phenomena typically associated with the spirits of dead people. GhostCat made a lot more sense if people heard bells ringing and smelled cat nip or found random sand piles.

I'd taken all the pieces and turned them over, but the puzzle in my mind wouldn't come together. We needed to talk to Miles and see if the ghost made him leave.

Unfortunately, I'd forgotten to look for the boxes Lucky stored in the basement to attempt a locator spell. Shady Grove was at least forty minutes from the public library. It was nearing sunset when Walter and I finished, and I wasn't about to enter a haunted, unlit bar alone after dark.

The next morning after breakfast, I headed over to Two Mules. Ben remained at the mansion, researching contractors and suppliers to call when we eradicated the spirits.

Maybe I'd notice more once the lights came on, but in the beam of my phone's flashlight, the basement looked like a massive room filled with garbage. Smaller than I'd expected, considering it ran below three buildings. Of course, it must have been divided, and all the stuff crammed in here made it seem smaller.

Lucky had mentioned selling the tables and stuff along with the bar, but I'd forgotten until entering this room. Wooden tables were stacked under the stairs. Giant wagon wheels that must have been decorative leaned against the wall behind them. I also spotted a giant ornate mirror, similar to the one hanging over the bar, and—was that a spittoon?

Several large wooden barrels lined the wall nearest the stairs. They were dusty, but someone had written on them. The one nearest me appeared to have a year stamped on the top, along with "Napa Valley" and other words that meant nothing. Maybe the manufacturer? These had to be wine barrels. I wondered if they were empty and, if not, how long did wine remain good buried underground in a place that froze every winter?

GhostCat crossed the floor ahead of me, jumped up on a barrel, and lay down, gazing at me with his unnerving stare. Now both eyes were green.

Remembering Pink's warning, I shivered. "It's okay. I'm looking for a sweatshirt. Lucky said I could use it to find a man who might have killed Leo. You know Leo, right?"

The cat didn't even twitch in response. His gaze bored into me as if he were trying to telepathically control me. At least he wasn't growling. When he didn't move, I presumed he would let me continue my mission.

After sweeping the beam of light around the floor, I turned my flashlight on the far corner. Like Lucky said, a pile of cardboard boxes was collecting dust. Once upon a time, the spider webs and dirt would have made me hesitant about exploring further. Now, a simple hand gesture made the boxes as clean as new.

The old tape opened easily beneath my fingertips. To my immense relief, the first box contained a navy blue sweatshirt with SUNY on the front. It was a men's size large, so I assumed it belonged to Miles.

Rather than dig into the rest of the box, I sent my magic looking for anything different—another size, or women's clothing, something to suggest the entire box didn't belong to Miles. Once satisfied, I folded the top flaps and examined my booty.

The sweatshirt's appearance as a perfectly ordinary article of clothing disappointed me, like I'd expected a forwarding address for Miles sewn inside.

Still, it should lead me to him. I couldn't wait to find out.

HALF AN HOUR LATER, I entered the mansion and spotted Walter watching TV with T. The screen played a gardening video, and my grandfather pouted in the corner of the couch, arms folded. When he saw me, he leaped to his feet.

"I'm so glad you're here! T is trying to bore me to death —again. He's watched this video at least three times."

On the screen, a man explained how to use new watering techniques to help plants thrive in unfriendly climates. I didn't understand a word of it, but I supported anything that helped my gardens flourish. We had several acres for T to explore his powers, and I was all for him experimenting.

I waved hello to T and told him I'd be in the ballroom until dinner. He agreed to send Pink my way if he saw him, but when Walter and I entered the room, my cat lounged on the piano bench in the sunbeam. Outside the windows, two men from the local gardening store installed bird feeders.

Spoiled cat.

Sitting down, I scratched his ears. He let out a purr and snuggled up against me. When he rolled over and put his feet in the air, I rubbed his belly while explaining everything I'd learned in the last few days.

"I don't understand how the bar can open," I said. "GhostCat let us in, sure, but will that continue if Ben tries to operate a business? What if GhostCat chucks everyone out, or worse? I don't know what he's capable of."

"You could try a spell to banish both ghosts," Pink said.

"Seems rude. Aren't we talking about a human being in pain? I'd prefer to save brute force as a last resort." I hesitated. "Besides, after that protection spell, I don't think I can."

"Then you need to help him," Pink said. "What do you know about Lucky?"

"She doesn't strike me as a killer," I said. "Besides, she had the place for over a year before she sold it. Would it take Leo that long to drive her away if she killed him?"

"Depends on how stubborn she is," Walter said.

"But she didn't leave because the bar was haunted. She gave up when her construction fund got stolen. Could the ghost have taken her money?"

"Normally, I would say no. With this ghost? It's possible. But she would have found it. Leo might shift items around using the same energy GhostCat used to attack you, but he couldn't carry anything to another location. If they hid her money, it should be in the building somewhere."

I shook my head. "Lucky seemed positive her ex-boyfriend took it. They never found him."

"Maybe Leo is mad at this bounder for besmirching his niece's honor and taking her dowry!" Walter punctuated this suggestion by striking a traditional dueling pose. "En garde!"

"There you go," Pink said.

"It was 2002, not 1802."

"Not the duel stuff. But if Leo was hanging around the bar, maybe he chased Miles away."

"Wouldn't that resolve his business?" I asked.

Walter returned to his normal stance. "We need to ask Miles what happened before he left."

"The way to save the bar is to hunt down a person who disappeared twenty years ago? Great. Easy peasy." I rolled my eyes.

Walter said, "Who said *you* have to find him? Hire a private investigator."

"I was thinking about a locator spell, but I'm not sure I can," I said.

"Oh, I used to love locating spells!" Walter clapped. "Can't believe I forgot. I used them to find my reading glasses."

"They were always on a chain around your neck," Pink muttered. "And, yes, Emma, you can do them. As Walter has illustrated, being able to find things is useful around the home."

Leaving them behind, I headed upstairs to my room. Since Walter loved locating spells, I grabbed his spell book first. It only took a minute to find something manageable. I scanned the list of ingredients, and all were in my regular supplies. Quickly, I gathered everything and returned to the ballroom.

Although everyone here knew my secret, I locked the door to avoid interruptions. I lit a stick of incense and waved it around the room, chanting words of protection and clarity. When I'd completed a full circle, I set the still-burning stick in a holder on the piano bench. Next, I spread Miles's hoodie on the floor in the middle of the room, then unfolded a map of the United States on top of it.

The idea was to have it direct me to the city and state where Miles lived now. Once I narrowed down the primary geographic area, I could print city and street maps and repeat the process. It would take time, but the extra step should pay off. Next, I placed a printout of Miles's newspaper picture beside the hoodie. It wasn't recent but gave me an image to focus on. Then, I walked around the sweatshirt and placed candles, creating a big enough circle to give myself room to navigate. The next step was to draw a line of sand around the candles to contain the energy.

After finishing the prep, I sat cross-legged in the circle and breathed deeply, inhaling the incense and opening my mind. The spell's words rolled off my tongue. After the incantation, I took a handful of sand and blew it across the map. It hung in the air for a moment before swirling above the map.

When the vortex settled, the sand shimmered, illuminating a small town near the New York/Vermont border. Exactly where Shady Grove was.

After everything we'd learned so far, it never occurred to me that Miles might not have fled very far. I'd expected the spell to light up Florida or maybe somewhere on the West Coast. But he was close enough that I might get an address tonight.

The smoke cleared, and a thin pink thread stretched through the air toward me. One end stopped directly in front of my face. The other went through the far wall.

"Do you see that?" I asked, passing one hand back and forth through the line. It remained intact. "Did I make that?"

"I do, and you did," Walter said.

"Can other people see it?"

"No," Pink said. "Not unless they see magic."

Walter said, "The real question is, where does it go?"

"To Miles, right? Let's follow it. You with me?"

"Yessss!"

The thread headed east toward Josie's bedroom. Chances were Miles wasn't hanging out in my house, so I ran upstairs to grab my keys, then headed for the driveway.

As I'd hoped, the thread came with me. Now it stretched around the mansion, pointing toward the woods,

Shady Grove, and beyond that, Vermont. Turning to check behind me, I saw nothing. As I moved, the magic spooled inside me.

Inside the car, I shivered. We'd reached the time of year when you couldn't walk around outside without a jacket. Good thing I had heated seats and steering wheel because I was way too excited to go back inside.

"What are you waiting for?" Walter asked.

"Just trying to warm up a bit," I said, rubbing my hands together. "Are you ready for adventure?"

"I was born ready."

We drove down the driveway and turned toward Shady Grove. "How long will this last? What if the thread vanishes before we get to Miles?"

"Those would've been excellent questions to ask your familiar. All I can tell you is, drive fast."

I suppressed a smile while subtly pressing on the accelerator. After about twenty-five minutes, the "Welcome to Shady Grove" sign appeared. Walter and I exchanged a look, but neither of us spoke. We were under the magic of the spell, and we made an unspoken promise not to detract from the moment.

Inside the town limits, I let my speed drop but kept my eyes glued to the thread. It seemed to point toward Town Hall. I tried to remember if there was a graveyard over there, but I only recalled the Town Square, a giant fountain, and other stops from last summer's treasure hunt.

The thread passed through Town Hall to Second Street, where it hung a right. Interesting. I slowed even more.

"Is it me, or is that thread darker?" I asked Walter.

"It's not you. It's thicker, too. We must be getting close."

Halfway down the block, the thread turned again. By

now, it was practically the size of a two by four. I parked the car, then looked up and let out a groan.

We sat in front of Two Mules.

"Maybe this isn't the end," Walter suggested. "Let's drive around and see if we pick it up on the other side."

My gut told me that option was too neat to be realistic, but I couldn't think of a better idea. We drove around the block. The entire time, the thread pointed directly from me to the bar. Front door, back door, didn't matter. We'd reached the end of the trail by arriving at the place where our quarry disappeared.

Since it was completely dark out, we couldn't go into the bar even if we wanted to. But I knew what we'd find: nothing. What went wrong?

"This makes no sense," I said. "Is Miles the ghost?"

"How can he be?" Walter asked. "He was alive when the hauntings started."

"Then the spell must have brought us to the rest of his clothes. There are boxes of them in there. What a stupid spell."

"It's not stupid," Walter said. "It could have worked."

"Sure, and I might learn to fly." I countered. "How does it help for a spell to take me to the place where I started?"

"Next time you go hiking, that spell is essential."

I tapped my fingers on the steering wheel, trying to figure out where I'd gone wrong. Maybe the sweatshirt was too old? Or maybe my power would only allow me to find clothes, and I'd only find Miles if someone handed me a picture of his current outfit.

Tears prickled the corners of my eyes. Sniffling, I tried to blink them away.

"It's okay. You did your best," Walter said. "The spell could've worked, and you never know unless you try."

"I'm a failure. Since the day we arrived, I've tried every-thing to help Ben buy this bar, and I'm completely useless. He needs an actual witch."

"None of that talk," Walter said. "You are an actual witch! We all have spells go wrong sometimes. Let's go home, and Pink can tell you about the time I tried to do a spell that would let me pitch for the Yankees."

A small chuckle escaped me. "That must have been something."

"Almost got me in a lot of hot water. He saved me. Come on. Sitting here isn't going to make you feel better. We'll think of something else."

Although he sounded upbeat, I felt terrible. Walter had been enjoying this chase, and I hated to ruin the moment by crying, but our exciting adventure turned into an epic disappointment.

With nothing else to say, I started the car and headed for home, trying not to let him see the tears streaming down my cheeks.

THIRTEEN

The next morning, I didn't see the point in going to Two Mules. The project seemed futile. Every day brought us closer to the frigid temperatures of winter in a building with no running water, lights, or heat. We were trying to help a ghost who had no interest in us. Maybe I should hit the internet and buy that fancy ghost-hunting equipment after all.

"What if we try a séance?" I asked during breakfast. "Heck, let's pick up a Ouija board."

Ben paused with a slice of bacon halfway to his mouth. "I can't tell if you're serious."

"I'm running out of ideas. Sitting in a dark room hoping Leo shows himself is getting frustrating."

"I feel bad taking up so much of your time," Ben said. "You should be here, running the B&B."

"It mostly runs itself." Literally, but he didn't need the specifics.

"Still." He paused. "You think a séance would work?"

Instead of answering, I addressed the air. "Walter! Where are you?"

My grandfather popped into view and reached for a piece of bacon. When his hand passed through it, he pouted. "Did you call me to gloat about your breakfast?"

"Of course not," I said, repeating his comment to Ben. "Have you ever attended a séance? As a ghost?"

"Now that you mention it, I've never been invited. Why? You want to do one?"

"At the bar."

"It wouldn't work," Pink said from behind me. "The purpose of a séance is to connect with spirits who are otherwise unable to interact with people in this world. This ghost is communicating, just not in the way you want."

I threw up my hand but relayed his comments to Ben.

"Maybe we should give up," he said miserably. "Once Darren's life insurance comes in, I'll buy a bar somewhere else. It'll only be a few more months and, as a bonus, he'd have hated that."

A wave of guilt hit me. Reaching over, I squeezed his hand. "We'll figure this out. Pink, you said it's possible GhostCat was being controlled by a talisman, right?"

"That would explain why he hurt you and Walter, and why Ben can see and hear him."

"Would the talisman be nearby?"

"Depends on the strength of the witch wielding it, but in most cases, yes."

"It's got to be in the bar," Ben said. "It should be easy to find. The upstairs is bare. Most of the kitchen has been cleared out. The only places to hide something are in the heat vents or the toilet tanks."

"Also, the basement."

"Isn't the basement empty?"

I realized that, although I'd updated Ben on the failed locator spell, I'd forgotten to tell him what I'd found. "One of the prior owners—or more—used it for storage and never emptied it. There's all the wooden furniture that goes with the Old Western theme, plus a bunch of dusty wine barrels and some cardboard boxes near the front wall. You could save a lot of money if you reused them."

"Someone put wooden barrels down there?"

"Yeah. I assumed to keep the wine cold. Why?"

"A full barrel weighs over five hundred pounds. You'd either need four guys risking their lives or a machine to get it down the stairs."

"Maybe they didn't have OSHA back then," I said. "Or they could be empty. Given the rest of the stuff down there, they might have been decorative."

"A basement full of furniture no one has touched in years seems like a good place to hide something."

"Agreed. Unfortunately, the talisman could look like almost anything," I said.

"Oh, yeah." He visibly deflated.

"While that's true, I expect you'll know when you see it," Pink said. "Usually, a talisman is bound with string or thread. You'll sense the magic."

"Say we find it. Then what?" Ben asked. "If we destroy it, do GhostCat and his companion disappear?"

"If there's any fabric or thread holding it together, I can track it to the witch who made it. The opposite of last night's locator spell."

"Maybe that's why the spell took us to the bar last night," Walter mused. "What if Miles planted the talisman?"

"Why would he do that?" I asked.

"Why would anyone create a spirit to scare people away from the local watering hole?"

He had a point.

"Once you trace the talisman to its creator, motive might become clear," Pink said.

"Hold on, Emma," Walter said. "I don't want you to do anything dangerous."

"I'll be careful. Ben, let's go find a talisman."

On the way to Two Mules, we stopped at a local hardware store and bought the largest freestanding battery-powered lights they had. Five of them. We'd never find anything wandering around in the dark, holding our phones in one hand. On the way to the register, Ben grabbed a headlamp. I did the same.

We loaded everything in the Porsche before Ben went back for extra batteries. Ten minutes later, we were on our way.

Once I parked in the rear lot, we adjusted our matching headlamps. I was starting to feel like a real ghost hunter.

Ben gripped my hand and squeezed before we got out of the car. "Thank you."

"Don't thank me yet."

GhostCat met us at the back door. That was new. He moved in and around my feet, looking up and meowing. I crouched down.

"What's going on?" Ben asked.

"Good question. What's wrong, GhostCat?"

GhostCat meowed again, and I scratched behind his ears. "Were you bothered by the magic last night? Sorry about that. We didn't mean to disturb you. We were trying to find the man who murdered Leo so he can rest in peace."

GhostCat gazed into my eyes as if trying to do mind control. His eyes were back to green and yellow.

"Do you know who killed him? If we bring Pink back, can you tell him?"

In response, GhostCat darted away. Fickle cats.

"Maybe he's starting to like you," Ben said.

"If he likes me, he should help."

"Sure, but how much help is a cat when opening a bar?"

"Lots, if you had mice." I shuddered. "Let's be glad for one problem we don't have."

"I suspect we have Grace and Floyd to thank for that. They have an interest in keeping the entire building rodent-free. If this place were free-standing, we'd be having a different conversation."

"A different conversation, outside, very far away," I joked.

GhostCat returned. When I met his eyes, he opened his mouth in a silent meow.

"What's that?" I asked him.

Instead of answering, GhostCat darted through the doorway, dashing right through Ben. He let out a yelp of surprise. "What's going on?"

The cat returned before I could respond. Another silent meow, then he raced away again.

"GhostCat is trying to tell us something," I said.

"He might be leading us to our deaths," Ben replied. "Wasn't that the threat?"

It was, but I didn't sense any danger. I followed GhostCat through the kitchen and across the attached storage room. He stopped at the door leading to the basement.

"Everything's fine," I told Ben.

My friend snorted. "Don't say I didn't warn you."

Frozen with indecision, I watched GhostCat pace back and forth in front of the basement door.

"Should I open the door?" I asked.

"Can't he walk through it?"

"He can, but he isn't."

GhostCat paused every few steps to stare at the doorknob. After three or four such passes, he reared up on his back legs to paw at it.

"If he wanted to hurt us, he could toss me out like before," I said. "He also had plenty of chances to push one of us down the stairs the other day."

"Is that supposed to be comforting?"

"In my head, it sounded better."

"Why do you think he's doing this?" Ben asked.

I shrugged. "He could've sensed the energy from my locator spell. It didn't do what we wanted, but it was still magic. Maybe he understands I want to help Leo? No idea, but I don't believe in looking a gift cat in the mouth."

Carefully, standing as far back as possible, I reached out and opened the door a crack. GhostCat slipped through the wood before the gap was even two inches wide. Before following him, I flipped on my headlamp and shone it down the stairs. The cat was gone.

Then he jumped into my beam, meowed again, and zoomed away.

"What do you want to do?" I asked.

"I hadn't planned on playing cat charades. Do we trust him?"

"Pink said they negotiated a truce. I don't think he would have let me come here if GhostCat still posed a danger. You remember how worried he was before our first trip here?"

"True, but we have no idea what could be lurking in the shadows down there."

"Good thing we bought these trusty headlamps."

GhostCat peeked at us through the still-open door before heading back down the stairs. He wasn't being subtle. Any minute, he'd drag me into the basement by my pant leg.

Ben ran a hand through his dark hair. "I don't like this, but we need to check. Whatever he wants to show you could be important. Just be careful."

When we entered the staircase, GhostCat bounded to the top before dashing back down. While I wasn't convinced he knew where to find a magical talisman, he believed something important lay down here.

At the bottom of the stairs, GhostCat raced away again. This time, he jumped on the second wine barrel and sat.

"Great. He wants a glass of chardonnay." I threw up my hands. The day had barely begun, and I was ready to go home and take a bubble bath.

GhostCat meowed again. My headlamp's beam swept over every surface, taking in the exposed brick walls, the packed dirt floor carrying bits of sawdust tracked from upstairs, and the ghostly cat who, even now, glared at me from where he sat on one of the wine barrels. If I hadn't seen him upstairs earlier, I'd think he'd been waiting there for me since I borrowed Miles's sweatshirt.

It seemed odd that he would return to the same one. There were no windows down here, so it wasn't a spot for catching a sunbeam.

GhostCat met my eyes, and a chill went down my spine. He was sending me a message.

"There's something about that barrel," I said. "GhostCat guards it. Both times I've been down there, he's sat on it and glared at me like he's trying to make me hear his thoughts."

"Maybe it is the talisman?" Ben said doubtfully. "They hid it in plain sight?"

"Interesting theory. The barrel itself isn't magic, as far

as I can tell." If Pink was wrong about me sensing magic, we were in trouble. "Something could be inside."

"Those are almost three feet tall. How big a talisman are we looking for?"

I considered that for a minute before shaking my head. "It should be about the size of your standard voodoo doll—three or four inches. But if these barrels were here when the talisman was hidden, the witch could've taken advantage of them."

"You could fit a lot of money into one, too," Ben said. "Did Miles hide Lucky's missing money? Maybe the ghost stopped him from taking it, and he never came back."

As theories went, it wasn't the worst one I'd heard so far. "Either way, GhostCat wants us to look inside. Let's find something to open it with."

We did another sweep with our flashlights, but neither of us spotted any tools for removing hoops.

"Hold on," Ben said. "I've got a toolkit in my car. Nothing fancy, but there's a hammer."

"You want to break it open?"

"Do you have a better idea?"

I didn't. He headed upstairs while I explored the rest of the room. I closed my eyes, feeling with my power for any magical object in the area. Either the talisman was out of my range, or I didn't know how to find it.

Maybe it wasn't here at all. It could be under the wooden sidewalk outside or in the rain gutters for all we knew. If whoever controlled GhostCat was more powerful than we thought, the talisman might not even be in Shady Grove.

Running my hands over the surface of the barrel, I sought cracks or any catch that might open a hidden compartment big enough to store a talisman. There was nothing. Then I reached out with my magic. It flowed through the barrel and expanded into the wall beyond, finding pants and a shirt.

"What's behind this wall?"

Ben glanced at the stairs then toward the wall before answering. "The street, I think. Why?"

This wasn't the time to play coy with my powers. "I'm sensing clothes over here. It might be someone on the street, but I think we're too low."

"The barrel could have been used for storage." Ben knocked on the lid. The sound echoed.

My magical pull didn't feel like a stack of neatly folded clothes. I sensed something about the width of one shirt and one pair of pants. My magic found nylon. Two separate pieces. One was mostly a square with a couple of long pieces hanging off the side. The other, well, it was shaped like pants.

Ben put one hand on the top and cocked his head as if listening. "That's a pretty cool power. I don't sense anything. You ready?"

I nodded.

The hammer swung through the air. An angry thwack sounded when it hit the lid. A tiny crack appeared. Ben lifted the hammer above his head again, bringing it down soundly.

"One more good swing," he said.

The hammer cracked against the wood again. It splintered. Dust filled the air as the wooden pieces clattered to the ground. A pungent odor hit my nose, sending me reeling backward. It wasn't wine, though. When the dust cleared, a dead body lay before us.

FOURTEEN

For a long moment, Ben and I gazed at the poor person who'd been released from their wooden tomb. Based on the state of the body, whoever this was had been in there for many years. The smell made bile rise in my throat—the barrel must have contained the decomposition gases all this time.

Ben waved a hand in front of his face and coughed. He looked like he wanted to say something, then coughed again.

The stench was overpowering. I pointed at the stairs. The two of us headed for the sweet relief of fresh air.

Once outside, we took several deep breaths. Finally, Ben said, "Was that Leo?"

I shook my head. "I don't think so. He died in a hospital. Why would someone bring him here?"

"Then who is it?"

Suddenly, I understood why my locator spell brought me to the bar. It hadn't fizzled out like I thought. The magic brought me to Miles, exactly as I'd asked. Because we thought he'd run off, I hadn't considered that he might still be *inside the building.*

The first reported haunting didn't coincide with his disappearance, and there'd been no reason to doubt that he'd taken off, so I'd never connected the dots. But before Miles ran away, Lucky never got bad vibes from the ghost. Maybe after Miles died, his extreme pain allowed his spirit to take over the bar and run the original ghost off?

Lucky had been certain he'd stolen her money and fled town. Was it a cover-up? They broke up a couple of months before Miles disappeared, yet kept working together. Maybe she'd been biding her time, waiting for an opportunity to show him how she felt about the breakup.

We'd been looking at this all wrong. Leo died from a heart attack, like everyone said. I should have trusted my instincts.

Now, all the pieces fit: someone murdered Miles and buried him here. His spirit remained in the bar, seeking vengeance. He didn't want the bar to open until his murderer had been brought to justice.

Finding someone who had long been dead wasn't technically an emergency, but I dialed 911 rather than look up the non-emergency phone number for the police station.

The dispatcher, who introduced herself as Marie, seemed surprised to hear me calling from Two Mules. "I thought the old bar was closed. Isn't that place haunted?"

I laughed nervously. "We're not sure, but we found a dead body in the basement."

She gasped. "What happened? I'll send the paramedics right away."

"I don't think an ambulance is necessary. This guy appears to have been here quite a while. Years, even."

"What makes you say that?"

I couldn't tell her my locator spell strongly suggested this was Miles. The body was too badly decomposed for anyone to recognize him, especially a total stranger who had only seen pictures in the newspaper.

"We found him in an old barrel covered in dust. My friend told me this place has been empty for quite some time. But also, there's a lot less of him than there should be, if you know what I mean. And the smell is horrifying."

Marie muttered something under her breath. I decided not to ask her to repeat it. "I'll put in the call, but the sheriff is off today. We'll have to send our backup detective, and he's further out. Please don't touch anything until he arrives."

I wouldn't touch anything in that basement if Tom Hiddleston went down there. I thanked her and hung up.

"We found our ghost, huh?" Ben asked.

"I guess so. That must be who GhostCat was protecting."

As if he heard his name, GhostCat passed through the door and joined us outside. When he saw me, he rubbed his cheek against my leg and meowed.

Crouching slowly, I met GhostCat's gaze in what I hoped was a non-threatening manner. He meowed again. "I know things have been busy around here, and I'm sorry. The police are on their way. They'll take your friend for a proper burial. Thank you for helping us find him."

He meowed again. I glanced at Ben, who shrugged. "Sounds like a yes to me."

A car pulled into the small lot and took the only available space, behind Ben's truck.

"Is that the coroner?" I asked.

"Or a police officer, maybe. Let's see."

We walked toward the car, but paused when the front door opened and the driver emerged. TJ had returned.

"TJ, I'm sorry, but this isn't a good time for an interview. Ben will call you next week," I said.

"Oh, I know. I heard you found a body."

"How could you possibly know that? I mean, um, what? Who said that?"

"Nice try. I've got a police scanner," he said. "Finding a body here after all this time is newspaper gold! It explains everything!"

"That's absurd."

"So says you," TJ replied. "You're not a local. The residents of our small town might think otherwise."

He moved toward the back door, but Ben blocked him. "I can't let you any closer until the police arrive. You could destroy evidence."

TJ sighed. "Fine. I'll take pictures of the outside, but after the police leave, will one of you give me a statement?"

"What are you doing at my crime scene?" Tim's voice boomed behind me, making all three of us jump. He must have come through the front door, because he now stood in the open back doorway.

His presence sent TJ scurrying away like a rat, which made me smile. "Hey. Thanks for coming so fast."

"Emma, when I said we should go to a bar, this wasn't what I meant."

"I am very sorry we keep meeting in these situations," I said. "But it's good to see you. At least we agree I had nothing to do with this. I lived more than a thousand miles away when this man died."

"How do you know?" Tim asked.

Lowering my voice, I said, "We're pretty sure this is

Miles Levine, the bar employee who vanished in 2002. Come on, I'll show you."

"Let me guess—you can't tell me why you think that."

Instead of answering, I led the way through the bar to the basement door. "Some of his things are down there. Maybe you can get DNA off them."

"Great idea, thanks." He made a note on his pad. "Neither of you owns this place, right? Please tell me you're not trespassing."

"We have permission to be here," Ben said. "The town foreclosed a few years ago, but I'm thinking about buying. They said we could look around."

At the bottom of the stairs, Tim directed me and Ben to stand a few feet from the barrel and direct our flashlights and headlamps at the remains. It wasn't as good as daylight, but enough to confirm that this poor person had been dead a while.

He pulled on a pair of gloves, then snapped several photographs with his phone before calling someone to provide backup. Then he crouched down to get a closer look, all without sparing a glance for the two of us in the corner.

"Do you know how he died?" Ben asked once it looked like Tim had examined everything.

"We're assuming it was murder, but..." I shrugged helplessly.

"It's tough when someone has been dead this long. I don't see anything obvious like a bullet hole, but the body is damaged. It's possible he died by accident and someone put him in the barrel because they panicked. It'll take time to get the coroner's report. You think you know him?"

"Yes. Miles Levine, who managed this bar, disappeared in 2002."

Tim cocked his head toward Ben. "Can I ask questions in front of him?"

"You both know enough about my powers to speak freely. It'll make everyone's life easier."

"Great," Tim said. "Is Miles's ghost here? Is that how you know?"

I shook my head. "We haven't seen him. He's got a cat, though, who led us down here."

GhostCat had been sitting quietly on the floor this whole time, but now he glared at me as if taking umbrage to being called a pet.

"That must be this guy," Tim said. "Beautiful boy. But how could he be Miles's pet? Who feeds him?"

"No one," Ben said. "He's a ghost."

Tim did a double take. "Look at that. In the dark, I couldn't tell."

Ben looked at me. "Was I that cool when you told me about all this?"

"Tim's had a lot more time to get used to it," I said.

"I've, uh, seen Emma in action before. Her and her ghost," Tim said. "Back to this guy. What makes you think you know who he is?"

"We've been researching the ghost. Miles's name was the only one linked to a suspicious disappearance," I said.

"I should've known you'd be three steps ahead of me."

GhostCat moved from the third barrel to one on the end, but he continued to watch with that unnerving gaze. His eyes were once again both green.

"Did we miss anything?" I asked.

He shook his head and sneezed, which I took to mean that the other barrels didn't contain any other former bar employees. Then we went upstairs to give our formal statements in better light. Every time I glanced toward Ben, the powerful beam he held made me see spots. Tim wasn't faring much better.

By the time we finished our reports, the crime scene team had finished processing the scene. TJ still hovered, so Tim asked him to give an official statement, moving him toward the sidewalk as he did.

Ben and I waited in a corner near the front door, not sure whether we should stay, go, or run away and never come back. Tim didn't want me involved in violent crime investigations, but he might think of more questions.

"What now?" Ben asked.

"Now we need to redouble our efforts to connect with these spirits. GhostCat led us to the body, but he can't be the one who's filling the place with human moans. I hoped Miles would show himself after we found his body, but there's no sign of him. Is he shy? Afraid of cats? Did something happen so he *can't* talk to us?"

"If the human ghost isn't Miles, we need to know that, too."

Lifting my head to the ceiling, I called out, "Who's here? Miles, is that you? It's okay! We're here to talk."

In response, the chandelier in the middle of the room lit up. Before anyone could react, the lights flickered off, then on, then off again. A sound reverberated through the space, so loud my ears vibrated. It took a minute to even realize the sound was laughter.

Not a cat. A very real sound of human amusement coming from upstairs.

To my knowledge, no one was up there.

"Do you hear that?" I asked.

"Yes. Is it the police?"

"What would they find so funny? And why aren't they in the basement?"

"Two intelligent questions I can't answer," he said. "Also, I am baffled as to how the lights are flickering when there's no electricity. I suppose the police could get the electric company to turn it on for their investigation, but this fast?"

Another excellent, yet terrifying point. No one could have turned the chandelier on, because the lights weren't powered.

My first instinct was to run. The flashing lights seemed like a warning, especially when combined with the increasingly maniacal laughter. But I'd promised to help Ben open the bar, and he couldn't run it like this. If Miles's ghost had been content to hang out and watch TV all day like my grandfather, that would be different.

But first, I had to ask, "Have you had an electrician in here? Maybe they fixed it."

"Not yet. I want to make sure the structure is sound first. Now that I'm worried a ghost might magically set the building on fire, I'm less inclined to put myself on the line."

Could a ghost start a fire? A week ago, I would have unequivocally said no. But now, I wasn't so sure. "If Miles burns the building down, would you rebuild? Maybe the fire could burn out the spirits and leave you with a place to rebuild from the ground up."

"I don't have insurance yet, so no. We'd have to walk away."

If the ghost's end goal was to keep the bar closed, a fire seemed like an excellent means of achieving it.

Tim approached, gesturing vaguely upward with one hand. "Was the chandelier doing that before?"

"Only the first day we got here," Ben said. He failed to mention that it should have been impossible, a fact that I appreciated.

"What about the temperature? Is it always this cold?" He shivered and rubbed his arms.

Until he mentioned it, I hadn't noticed the growing goosebumps on my arms. The basement had been chilly, but that was how unheated basements were. Now I realized that his breath lingered in the air.

While the temperature outside wasn't exactly warm this time of year, it wasn't this chilly.

"Our ghost is back," I said.

Tim said, "Let's eliminate the regular possibilities first, for the sake of not ending my career. Could someone have bumped the A/C by mistake?"

"It hasn't been turned on yet. We're at the mercy of the elements," Ben said.

Thoughtfully, I watched the crime technicians work. "All these buildings are connected, right? Since we're trying to find a mundane answer, I wonder if anyone else experienced a power surge."

"There are three meters out back. I'm not sure our wiring would affect them," Ben said. "It can't hurt to ask, though. Do you want to talk to Floyd and Grace or stay here and answer questions for the police?"

Neither. I wanted to go home and take a bath. "I'll flip you for it."

A few minutes later, I headed outside. The setting sun bathed the street in a soft glow. It was at least ten degrees warmer here than inside.

Cocoa Channel would be even warmer, so I headed there first. Bells above the door welcomed me into the homey space. The delicious scents of chocolate, caramel, and vanilla filled the air. My stomach growled, reminding me I'd forgotten to eat lunch.

Grace sat at the register, flipping through a magazine.

When I walked in, she hopped to her feet.

"Emma! I was so worried when I saw the police cars. Are you okay?"

"I'm fine. Ben and I found something in the basement we wanted to get checked out, that's all." My voice cracked, and I realized how exhausted I was. Ghost hunting wasn't for the faint of heart.

Her eyes widened. "Like what?"

I swallowed. "It looks like someone died down there. Years ago."

She gasped. "That's terrible. You must feel awful. Hold on, let me get you something."

While she spoke, she opened a display case beside the register and pulled out a chunk of fudge. Without comment, she passed it over the counter. The first bite was heaven. By the second, I could've walked on air. Not even Josie's food perked me up so much. When Grace set a glass of water on the low counter to wash everything down, I leaned across and hugged her.

"Thank you. I didn't realize how much I needed that."

"Chocolate cures everything. Do you know what happened?" Grace asked. "Tell me everything."

"I don't have any details." Even if I did, I wasn't much for feeding the gossip mill. "That's not why I'm here. Do these three stores still have the same wiring? I mean, if there was a problem with the electricity here, would it affect the other two businesses?"

"No, it's different. When Grandfather divided it up, they separated everything."

"What about the upstairs?"

"One meter per building covers upstairs and downstairs. Why?"

"No reason," I said quickly. "Just wondering how diffi-cult it would be to get the lights working again."

"You must be upset if you're confusing me with an elec-trician." She smiled ruefully.

"Yeah. It's just... hard to find someone like that, you know? He—or she—died all alone."

"In the end, we're all alone," she said. "But I know what you mean."

"Everyone was right. The bar is cursed," I moaned. "Someone doesn't want us to open the bar."

She snorted. "That's not supernatural. That's Floyd."

"What?"

"That old coot hates the bar, always has."

This was news to me. "Oh, yeah? Why?"

"Last call is four o'clock in the morning. Floyd runs a bait shop, and that means he opens early. The early bird and the worm, you know? Back when Leo owned the place, he'd take his favorite patrons upstairs after closing time. They'd still be partying when Floyd opened in the morning. More than once he caught someone passed out in his doorway."

"Isn't that illegal?"

"Probably." She shrugged. "Mayor Banister—not the current one, her uncle—was said to look the other way for the right price, if you know what I mean."

Based on what I knew about the current mayor, hearing that corruption ran in the family didn't faze me. "Leo bribed him?"

"I didn't say that. But I didn't *not* say that, either. Anyway, when Leo passed, Floyd could barely hide his plea-sure. At one point, I wondered if he'd figured out how to trigger a heart attack. Ridiculous, I know."

Considering I'd thought the same thing earlier, it

seemed plausible. "How did he react when Lucky took over?"

"He was upset, but then he talked to her. They came up with an accord. After that, he grumbled but seemed okay. I never asked for details." Her head came up sharply. "You don't think Floyd killed someone in the bar to keep it from opening, do you?"

"I'd imagine if he killed someone as a warning, the body wouldn't have stayed hidden for twenty years."

Although I didn't want Grace to speculate on the person's identity, my comment was an oversimplification. Killing Lucky's bar manager and stealing her entire renovation fund sounded like a great way to keep the business closed.

"You may be right," she said. "It's been peaceful around here. Then you all started showing up, and Floyd's on a tear again. He submitted a proposal for the next town council meeting to make Shady Grove a dry town."

"Really? Can he do that?"

"If it passes, sure. But I suspect we have enough residents to vote against him. The meeting is next Wednesday. You and Ben should come."

"We absolutely will. Thank you for the information." On my way out, I saved the information to my calendar and texted Ben to tell him what I knew.

His reply came immediately.

> How far would Floyd go to keep the bar
> from opening?

FIFTEEN

After leaving Cocoa Channel, I went to question Floyd. The sign on his door said Bait & Switch would be open until three, but the store was locked. No lights were on inside. I wish I'd noticed earlier; I could've asked Grace if it was common for him to close in the middle of the day.

Then again, I hadn't noticed whether the store was open when we arrived. He could have taken a day off to go fishing, for all I knew. Maybe the stress of finding a dead man made me see suspicious behavior where there wasn't any.

For now, I told Tim what I'd discovered before heading home. He'd be mad if I tracked down Floyd's home address and questioned him alone, and while I might still do that, I wanted to check with my supernatural companions first.

Back at the mansion, I sat down with Walter and Pink to ask for ideas.

Josie brought me a mug of coffee before sitting beside me with her own. Pink and I brought her up to speed. She took it all in with wide eyes. "I understand your confusion."

I tossed up my hands. "Did the ghost kill that man? Is that man the ghost? Either way, why won't he show himself?"

"I thought you said it wasn't a ghost," she said.

"We don't know what he is. At first we thought the spirit was a ghost who was so traumatized that his pain transcended the veil between worlds. Considering someone murdered Miles and stuck him in a wine barrel, then pretended he ran away, that makes sense. But unless he transformed himself into a cat, we haven't seen any sign of him."

"Ghosts can't do that," Walter informed me. "At least I can't."

"To my knowledge, no one can," Pink said. "It's possible Miles moved on, and he's not the one haunting the bar at all. Unfortunately, the only way to know that is to speak with him or ask GhostCat."

"GhostCat led us to the body, but I don't know how much help he can be," I said. "Did you put a spell on him?"

"I neutralized the anger controlling him. It wasn't his, which made it relatively simple for me to funnel it away from him and let it dissipate."

"Miles's anger." We'd come full circle. "Lucky must've killed him. He dumped her for another woman. Maybe she knew he was planning to run away—or maybe he stole the money, and she caught him before he left. We should talk to her again."

"Do you know if anyone notified her that Miles's body was found?" Josie asked. "If not, you've got the perfect opening."

"You're right." Standing up, I grabbed my keys. "Want to come?"

"Shotgun!" Walter yelled, racing past us through the wall that led to the front door.

I glanced at Pink. "You in?"

"No, thank you. I've had enough of car rides. Besides, she would think it incredibly strange if you showed up holding a cat."

"Hold on a minute," Josie said. "Ever since you asked me to help find the person who killed Ben's stepfather last month, I've felt terrible. You're out there every day, risking your life to help people in need, and I cower back here in my kitchen. Now that we've gotten to know Ben, the guilt is even harder to bear."

"You have absolutely no reason to feel bad," I said. "You're dealing with your own issues. This is scary stuff, and no one expects you to risk your life."

"Well, yeah, but I'm also feeling safe here and becoming more confident. As long as my name doesn't wind up in the papers, I want to help."

My brow wrinkled as I thought about her words. "You want to interrogate Lucky?"

"Not exactly. Wait here." Josie headed into the kitchen. When she returned, she held what looked like a container of chocolate chip cookies. "Take her some of these."

My eyes widened. "Please tell me those are what I think they are."

"I've been experimenting. I put a truth spell on them. They taste good, but I don't know if they *work*."

I didn't hesitate before grabbing one. "What happens? If I try to lie, do the words get stuck? Or do you know I'm lying?"

"Good question." She picked up a cookie and broke it in half. After holding a piece out to me, she took a bite. "My name is Josie, and I love my ex-husband with all my heart."

I snorted. "Looks like you can speak lies."

"Did you sense anything?"

"Nope, but I'm not the one who did the spell. This isn't tied to my magic. Let me try." I bit into the cookie. It tasted exactly like a chocolate chip cookie. "My name is Emma, and this is an oatmeal raisin cookie."

Josie's eyes widened. "When you said your name, you glowed green. When you said the cookie bit, your aura turned red."

"It works!" My joy couldn't have been more if I'd been the one to come up with and master the spell. A working truth serum was priceless.

"Guess I'm coming with you, after all." She took off her apron and smoothed her hair. "I can't wait to tell Walter to sit in the back seat."

We spent the drive discussing how to approach Lucky. Even after twenty years, she'd be upset to learn about Miles's death. But if she'd been the one to hide him in the basement, she might also be dangerous.

"Make it easy," Walter suggested. "Hand her a cookie, wait for her to take a bite, and ask her if she killed him."

"What if she doesn't answer?" I asked.

"Then make her clothes move until she does. Come on, you're a thread witch! Be creative."

"I'm not sure the spell works if someone is coerced into speaking," Josie said after I repeated his idea. "I'd rather not find out."

"Agreed," I said.

"Let's keep it simple. We go in, we offer condolences, we ask if she ever suspected he didn't run away, and we see what she says," Josie said.

"You guys are so boring," Walter complained.

"It's perfect," I said.

"Thanks. From the look on your face, I don't want to know what Walter thinks," Josie said.

"Ask Lucky about her uncle, too," Walter said. "In case she killed him to inherit the bar."

I'd abandoned the "Leo was murdered" theory as soon as we spotted Miles's body, but it couldn't hurt to cover all the bases.

By the time we reached this consensus, I was parking in front of Lucky's house. She sat on the front porch, rocking in the swing. A breeze ruffled her hair. She stared into space, giving no sign that she'd noticed us.

When we were halfway up the driveway, I called her name. She jumped and turned toward me. At this distance, I noticed how red her eyes were. Taking the cookie container from Josie, I moved toward her. "I'm so sorry, Lucky. It looks like you heard."

"He's been gone twenty years." She sniffled. "I shouldn't feel this bad."

"You should feel exactly what you feel," Josie said before introducing herself. "You thought he left you. Being dead is a different loss."

"He still left me," she said. "We broke up months before he died. But part of me thought he'd come back."

"I know it's not nearly enough," I said, holding out the box, "but we brought you cookies. Did the police tell you what happened?"

She shrugged but reached for a cookie and examined it before taking a small bite. "They told me the basics. I didn't need the details. I can't imagine why anyone would want to hurt him. Everyone loved Miles."

"Do you remember him arguing with anyone before he disappeared?" I asked.

"Like the ghost?" Lucky laughed hollowly, then finished

the cookie. "Maybe I should have taken the rumors more seriously."

"There was nothing you could do," I said, my eyes on Josie. She nodded slightly. Lucky was telling the truth. "Someone has been haunting the bar for years, and they never had a conversation with anyone that I'm aware of."

"I should've tried harder to find him. Maybe if I'd pushed, the police would've found the truth. Now it's been twenty years. We'll never know who did this."

"Did Miles have any enemies?"

"Uncle Leo, but that's no help. He'd been dead for a year." She sighed. "I don't think Uncle Leo would come back as a ghost to kill my ex-boyfriend."

"Is it possible he didn't want anyone else to run the bar?"

"Nah. Leo wasn't that kind of guy. He'd always been delighted by my interest."

"What about his ex-wife?" I asked. "Is it possible she killed Leo, and Miles found out about it?"

Lucky thought for a minute. "You know, Aunt April and I never got along. I'd be happy to throw her under the bus if there was any possibility she did it. But she and her sister toured Europe to celebrate their dual divorces before Leo passed. She wasn't here."

Josie and I exchanged a look. Her eyes told me that Lucky was still speaking the truth. She didn't have anything to do with Leo's death, or Miles's, and she didn't think her aunt did, either.

"The police are combing the bar for clues," I told her. "It might not be too late. It's possible the killer made a mistake."

She laughed hollowly. "I wish you luck. And you know how I feel about luck."

SIXTEEN

The next morning, Tim cleared us to reenter Two Mules, so Ben and I made an appointment with an engineer to make sure the building was structurally safe. Shady Grove suffered an earthquake last summer, which affected several buildings on nearby Main Street. Between that and the yearly snowstorms putting stress on the roof and the inexplicable drafts, Ben wanted to see exactly how much work the bar needed.

If an inspection revealed major problems, he preferred to know before it was too late. Saratoga Springs might be a bit of a drive, but worth the extra distance to buy a non-haunted bar without a crumbling infrastructure.

Our meeting was at nine. By nine-thirty, Ben and I had combed every inch of the bar on our own, gone on a coffee run, and swapped most of our best college stories. No sign of the engineer. Ben sent four texts and called, with no response.

"Are you sure about the time?" I asked at quarter after ten.

"I confirmed it yesterday," Ben said. "Hopefully, he'll be

here soon. I wanted to swing by the superstore after he finished."

"Go," I said. "I can wait here."

"Are you sure?" He gazed around. "You don't mind being alone?"

"Maybe Miles will talk to me if we're alone," I said. "Besides, we might as well be productive. You do what you need to. I'll start cleaning."

"Cleaning supplies are on my list," Ben said. "But there's no sense spending a lot of money before I know if this place is worth buying."

"Whatever you buy, you'll need to clean it, right? It's pointless for both of us to sit here, draining our phone's batteries. I'll text you if this guy shows."

Ben looked like he wanted to argue more, but sitting in a semi-lit room with no electricity, empty coffee cups, and our dwindling batteries didn't get him any closer to opening his business. Instead, he gathered the garbage so he could toss it in the dumpster out back on his way to the car.

"Ah, alone at last," I said to the empty room.

As a hearth witch, cleaning a massive room didn't require any electricity. No supplies, either. When Ben returned, this place would sparkle—and he never needed to know it took me less than thirty seconds.

With a wave of my arms, the dirty streaks on the wall vanished. I flicked my wrist and watched the dust evaporate from the bar stools. A rush of power gathered up all the dirt and sawdust into a neat pile, as if I'd spent twenty minutes sweeping.

"Now that's more like it," I said.

A voice from the doorway made me jump. "You the owner?"

Spinning around, I came face-to-face with a lean man who looked to be in his sixties. Gray hair, built like a scarecrow, wearing loose jeans, a buttoned up flannel shirt, and work boots. He didn't look particularly friendly, but nothing in his expression suggested he'd witnessed my spells.

"I'm Emma. Ben stepped out, but he'll be back soon. You must be the engineer."

"Jared." He grunted. "When I make an appointment, I expect people to be here."

Reminding him that the appointment had been over an hour ago would not help this meeting, but I nearly had to bite my tongue off with the effort. "I'm very sorry. Let me send him a message."

"First, he's not here. Now you want me to wait around while you play with your phone? Listen, Lady, don't waste my time."

Shady Grove is a small town, I said to myself. There weren't a lot of people available to do this work. All I needed was to get through this one conversation, then Ben would come back, and I could leave.

"I'll show you around," I said through gritted teeth. "We can start here, then I'll take you upstairs."

"Listen, I don't need no tour. Let me poke around. If you want to help, get me some coffee." He'd barely finished speaking before he walked over to the wall and started pressing on it. I'd been dismissed.

"The kitchen isn't operational," I said. "Gas, water, and electric are off until we verify that it's safe to turn them on."

"There's a shop down the street," he said without turning around. "I'll take a latte, extra foam, whole milk. None of that non-fat, decaf nonsense you millennials like."

"Should I pick you up some avocado toast?" My sarcasm

dripped from every word, but Jared didn't notice. As much as I hated to be rude, this guy rubbed me the wrong way. I couldn't wait to be out of his presence—even if that meant turning into his errand girl.

"No, thanks. It's not professional to eat on the job."

Two steps outside, I texted Ben.

> Engineer is here. Total jerk. I'm doing a coffee run.

> I'll be right there!

> Don't rush on my account. I get the impression he works better alone.

> What if the ghost gets him?

> He deserves it.

Since I didn't want Jared to catch me standing in front of the building texting, I put my phone away and headed to the coffee shop. With its red-and-white-striped awnings over the bright windows, On What Grounds? looked warm and inviting.

The long line inside the coffee shop gave me time to clear my head and remind myself that, as soon as Ben returned, I could hang out with Grace until Jared finished. The bar was spotless, we couldn't talk to ghosts until the engineer left, and I didn't have anything else to do. This guy didn't get to mess up my day.

By the time I returned to the bar with the drinks, I'd restored most of the good mood Jared shattered with his abrupt manner.

Walking from the brightly lit street into the semi-darkness made me shiver. *Please let this inspection go well.* Being able to see would make a world of difference.

The room looked exactly as I'd left it, except without an engineer. I hoped he hadn't left without talking to Ben—especially after demanding I buy him coffee.

"Hello?" my voice echoed around the empty room. "Jared?"

No answer. A full structural analysis should take longer to complete than the ten minutes or so I'd been gone. "Ben? Anyone here?"

Still nothing. Maybe he couldn't hear me. After poking my head in the kitchen, walk-in fridge, and massive pantry to verify that Jared hadn't gotten stuck anywhere, I checked the back parking lot. A massive blue truck sat out there. It didn't belong to me or Ben, so Jared must be around some-where. After a glance at the empty cab and surrounding area, I concluded he must be upstairs. This was starting to get irritating. I'd come to help Ben rid the place of ghosts, not play hide-and-seek with the rudest man in town.

Since my coffee was now empty, I tossed the cup in the dumpster beside the door before heading inside. Weird that he wasn't making any sound up there—I expected to hear banging or at least footsteps on the ceiling. The place wasn't soundproofed.

At the base of the stairs, I stopped. Red letters dripped blood down the wall. *GO AWAY!*

A gasp escaped me. Did Jared do this? No one else was here. But why?

Then my gaze dropped, and the gasp turned into a scream.

Jared lay crumpled on the floor.

SEVENTEEN

Oh, no. Not again.

Racing to Jared, I dropped to my knees. "Are you okay? Help!"

No answer. Not even an eyelid flutter. I scrambled for his wrist.

When I found a pulse beneath my fingertips, an enormous sigh of relief escaped me. He was alive. Unconscious, but breathing shallowly. There didn't have to be another death in this bar. Yanking my phone out of my pocket, I dialed 911.

Dispatcher Marie recognized my voice. That couldn't be a good sign.

"Hold on. This about the guy in the basement? I sent an officer yesterday. You mean he never showed up?"

"Um, no. He came. This is a separate incident," I said. "Someone fell down the stairs. He's breathing but unconscious."

"Okay, the paramedics are on their way. I'm also sending a police officer, don't you worry." She paused. "Did you see what happened?"

"No, I was getting coffee," I said. "Ben—the guy who's thinking about buying the place—left before Jared got here."

"Did you see anyone when you got back?"

"Just some giant creepy red letters on the wall." Looking at the words sent a chill down my spine, but I couldn't avoid them. "It says 'Go Away.'"

"It might be safer for you to wait outside."

"I realize Jared and I are strangers, but I'd feel better staying with him." If the ghost attacked him, it was partially my fault. I couldn't leave him alone.

"That's kind of you. If you hear anything suspicious, get out. The ambulance is on its way. We're going to pick up one injured party, not two."

"Promise," I said.

Sirens wailed in the distance before Marie and I hung up.

Not knowing what else to do, I texted Ben to tell him what happened. It was chilly in the stairwell, so I used my power to call warmth into Jared's clothing. At my request, the threads loosened to make him more comfortable. I didn't dare risk moving him in case he'd hurt his spine, but it was something.

GhostCat appeared in the opening at the top of the stairs.

I met his two-colored gaze in what I hoped was a non-threatening manner. He meowed. "You didn't see what happened, did you?"

Unsurprisingly, he just looked at me.

"Did Jared slip? Earthquake? You didn't push him, did you?" I asked. "Anyway, I called an ambulance. They'll be here any minute."

He meowed.

"Did Miles do this?"

My only response was a derisive look. Yes, it felt like a dumb question to me, too, but I'd thought the incidents would stop once we found Miles's body. I couldn't believe this was happening. If I'd had any idea Jared might be in danger, I would've stayed with him, despite his demeanor.

The back door creaked open. I went to see if Ben had returned, but unfortunately, it was TJ. Again.

"Is it me, or do you keep popping up when you weren't invited?"

"Just doing my job," he said.

"Great. Do it somewhere else." This guy bugged me. Was there so little news in this town he needed to stalk the bar? Did he have a way of speaking to Miles's ghost? Maybe *he knew* something was going to happen, but couldn't admit it. Or maybe he was the one causing it, which made it in my best interests to keep a healthy distance.

Food for later thought.

I was still trying to figure out how to forcibly eject TJ from the premises without using magic when Ben arrived. "Emma, what's going on? Sorry it took so long. Some jerk cut me off in the parking lot and raced in here like there was a fire. I had to park on the street."

"Ben, you remember Some Jerk, right?"

TJ grinned as if happy to accept the title.

Leaving him, I took Ben to the stairwell. On the way, I lowered my voice and explained what happened. His face grew pale when he saw Jared.

"I called an ambulance."

"It was pulling into the lot when I got to the door," he assured me. "How's our victim?"

"Breathing," I said. "Doesn't appear to be bleeding, thankfully. He might have been lucky."

"I hope so," Ben said.

Pounding feet took my attention back to the doorway. A second later, two paramedics rushed by before dropping to examine Jared.

"Did he hit his head?" the man asked.

"I didn't see him fall," I said. "But he's unconscious, so I think so."

The space at the bottom of the stairwell was getting cramped, so I stepped back into the kitchen. Not knowing what else to do, I paced. Back door to front door, to bottom of the stairwell, repeat.

A man's voice called me to the front. "What's going on in there?"

The voice sounded familiar, so I followed it through the bar and out the double doors. Floyd stood on the sidewalk, scowling. As soon as he saw me, he put his hands on his hips. "There's an ambulance blocking the driveway!"

"Sorry about that," I said. "Our engineer fell down the stairs."

His breath caught. "Jared? Is he okay?"

"I'm not sure. The paramedics are with him. Have you been here all day? Did you hear anything or see anyone coming or going from the bar?"

Floyd tilted his head as if thinking. After a long moment, he said, "I saw you leaving. I didn't see you come back, then the paramedics arrived."

"Where were you after I left?" I asked.

"In my shop, where else? Some kids turned the sporting goods into a disaster earlier. Took me most of the morning to put everything back. When I finished sweeping and returned the broom to the back room, I saw flashing lights. You don't think I spend all day with my nose pressed to the windows, do you?"

"No, of course not. Do you know if Jared had any health issues? Something that might cause him to lose his balance or fall?"

"When you get to be my age, we all have balance issues. Some people more than others."

I took that as a yes. "You didn't hear him fall?"

"Nope. Not that I would. Got my whole place sound-proofed back in the '80s."

"You got a sporting goods store soundproofed?"

He snorted. "I soundproofed the store next to the loudest business in town. It was cheaper than moving, believe it or not. Got a good deal. Those bar parties were terrible, people waking me up at all hours of the night. I was relieved when I heard old Leo and his wife were divorcing. Hoped to talk to them into selling the space to some nice omelet bar. A place where people could come for an early breakfast before getting some bait and tackle, then head out for a morning fishing trip." His face grew wistful, as if picturing the scene. "That would have been great."

"It sounds lovely."

"Yeah, well, it never happened. I need to get back. If he wakes up, tell Jared I'll check on him this afternoon."

As he turned and walked back toward his store, I wondered again how much Floyd hated working next to a bar. He easily could have slipped out his back door, through the parking lot, and upstairs without me knowing. Since only three of us used the back lot, no one would have seen him. He could have been waiting upstairs when Jared arrived.

Floyd seemed to consider the engineer a friend, but I barely knew either of them. The whole thing could be a show. Did Floyd hate loud neighbors enough to push a man down the stairs? Maybe he asked if Jared would wake up because Floyd didn't want to be named as the one who pushed him.

Back in the bar, I found Tim talking to Ben. He turned to me. "Those letters on the wall—were they there before TJ showed up?"

I tilted my head at him. "You think TJ pushed Jared? I wondered the same thing earlier."

"He's been known to pump up a story for not being juicy enough on its own." Tim shook his head. "The Shady Grove crime beat isn't interesting enough for him."

"That's absurd! What about journalistic integrity?"

"He has none," Ben said. "His dad was a brilliant reporter when I was a kid. Now Hal runs the paper, and his son embellishes the stories. It's sad."

"Well, I don't know TJ or whether he would push a man down the stairs to sell more papers, but I found Jared—and the warning—right before he arrived. Doesn't mean he wasn't lurking. He's here more than he should be."

Ben said, "He's obnoxious, but that doesn't mean he might be a killer."

"Heavy emphasis on 'might,'" Tim said. "We don't know anything yet, but those words *are* a crystal-clear message. They're still wet, so whoever pushed Jared must have finished right before you found them. Did you see anyone?"

I thought about it, but I'd been too busy fuming about how Jared treated me to notice my surroundings. Finally, I shook my head. "Sorry. Unless you want an alibi for Julie at the coffee shop, I can't help."

"Can you think of anyone who was upset about you coming in here and making changes?"

"Floyd. He's apparently a friend of Jared's."

"You'd think, if they're friends, he'd ask Jared to fail our inspection instead of killing him."

"Maybe he did," Tim said. "Floyd asks, Jared refuses, they argue, Floyd shoves his friend down the stairs. Stranger things have happened. Anyone else?"

Not exactly a "someone," but we both knew something didn't want the bar to reopen.

Finally, Ben said, "I know you can't put in your report that a ghost made Jared fall, but maybe something spooked him?"

Tim made a note on his pad. "It's possible. A lot of things could cause a person to fall down the stairs that have nothing to do with ghosts or being scared."

"When I came back from the coffee shop, GhostCat was at the top of the stairs. I don't want to believe he did this, but maybe..." I trailed off as I realized that, even with all his other impressive feats, the ghostly feline probably couldn't write in English. "We think there's another ghost. Someone who lets the cat do his dirty work and doesn't want to be seen."

"That explains the dead man in the barrel," Tim asked. "I'm still working to confirm his identity. Miles wasn't married, and he doesn't have any family in this area. We got his last name from the old owner and not much else. If he is who you say, she's our most likely suspect."

"Lucky didn't do it," I blurted. "But, uh, you'll have to trust me on that."

Shaking his head, Tim made another note on his pad. "I'll get supporting evidence. Thanks for the info, both of you."

"If you want to thank me, figure out what happened. I can't stand the thought of anyone else getting hurt because of me." With thunder clouding his face, Ben strode back inside the bar.

I wanted to comfort him, but Tim stopped me.

"Tell me what you know about that guy. Could he have come back while you were gone?"

I shook my head. "No. He went to the big box store, and that's at least half an hour away."

"You sure?"

"Am I sure he left before Jared arrived? Yeah, I watched him go. His car wasn't in the lot when I got back. Ask if he bought anything; he'll tell you."

He watched me intently. "You trust the guy?"

"He's never given me any reason not to," I said. "Ben's wanted this for years. It wouldn't make sense to sabotage himself."

Tim nodded. "Agreed, but I prefer to investigate every angle."

He turned to go, but I called him back. "What if Jared doesn't wake up?"

"Based on what you've told me? Then I'll have to figure out how to arrest a ghost for murder."

EIGHTEEN

Before Tim left, the techs took a sample of the blood on the wall and photographed everything. Then he gave me permission to clean up. Instead, I went upstairs to examine the area where Jared fell. Whatever I expected to find, it wasn't there. No scuff marks, not even footprints. Nothing but that ugly orange rug and more traces of sawdust that hadn't been cleaned up when I swept downstairs.

GhostCat walked over and sniffed my fingers. I smiled and scratched his head. "You're a good boy. I'm glad we worked out that little misunderstanding before."

In response, the cat sneezed and walked away, tail head high. After my first visit to the bar, there was no doubt in my mind that GhostCat *could* knock someone down the stairs if he wanted—after all, he landed me in the hospital and melted my phone. But I didn't think Pink would let me come here if he weren't one hundred percent positive that GhostCat no longer posed a threat.

There was also the small matter of the letters written on the wall in blood. Even if GhostCat could have gotten blood somewhere, how would he lug it in here and write with it? Could a ghost make blood letters appear?

Shaking my head, I went back down to examine the letters. Still shiny. An involuntary shudder went through me.

"Creepy, huh?" Ben asked.

I jumped about a foot at the sound of his voice. "They would be less disturbing if I knew where the blood came from. Jared wasn't bleeding."

"Do you think someone pushed him and cut their hand to write the letters?"

"That's more plausible than GhostCat doing it." I shook my head helplessly. "We're never going to figure this out. I'm useless."

"Don't beat yourself up. We've been working all hours of the day to appease a twenty-year-old ghost that neither of us can see or talk to. I should find another place. A friend of a friend heard about a bar in the Adirondacks that might be for sale soon."

The Adirondack mountains were almost an hour away when not contending with New York weather. "Don't give up. We'll see what the police find out. But for now, let's finish up and take the night off. Like you said, we've been working around the clock, and Josie's cooking a feast."

We took pictures of the bloody letters before a snap of my fingers returned the wall to its normal state. Removing the visible threat should have made me feel better, but negative energy hung in the air.

Ben took a flashlight and walked the entire structure again while I used my magic to probe for supernatural activity. I barely knew what I was looking for, and of course, I didn't find it. Part of me longed for an electromagnetic energy reader.

When he finished, we locked up and headed home. Halfway back to the mansion, Tim called. I took the call through my dashboard. "Do you miss me already?"

"Are you home? I'd like to drop by for a few minutes."

"You're not planning to arrest any of us, are you?" I tried to keep my tone light, but in the few months we'd known each other, both Josie and I had been under suspicion for crimes we didn't commit.

"I guess I deserved that. No, I need to talk to you about the bar. Also Ben, if he's around."

"Sitting right beside me," I said. "I guess that means it's not a social call?"

"Unfortunately not, but I am pleased to say I'm not currently investigating any of your friends."

"Wonderful! In that case, come on over. Dinner's at six. I'll be home in about ten minutes."

When he spoke again, a smile filled his voice. "I'd like that, thanks."

After we hung up, I called Josie to let her know to expect one more for dinner. The rest of the way, Ben and I tried to guess what the detective might want to tell us. Did he catch the person who'd pushed Jared? Did they identify Miles's killer? If Jared knew his attacker, it could be a quick arrest once he woke up.

Back home, the first thing I did was check my reflection in the mirror over the desk in the foyer. Yikes. My clothes never wrinkled, which kept me looking fresh most of the time. Too bad my hair didn't have the same magic. I could, however, smooth it down in the bathroom and pull it back. My tinted lip gloss also needed refreshing. By the time Tim arrived, I looked much better.

He looked nice in the suits and ties he wore as a detective, but when I took his coat, I caught a whiff of aftershave.

His face was free of the stubble I'd expect this late in the day, and his hair was freshly slicked back. This might not be a social call, but it was nice not to be the only one making an effort.

"Dinner isn't ready yet, but if we're going to talk about the case, we should sit in the dining room. It'll be more comfortable for all of us. Ben is in there getting drinks."

"Thanks. We definitely want to sit down for this."

"Detective, nothing you tell me is going to be more unbelievable than the things I see every day." Although my words sounded confident, I waited until we'd settled into our chairs before continuing. "What's going on?"

"Jared woke up."

"I'm glad to hear that," Ben said.

"Well, that's a relief. How is he? Don't tell me he doesn't remember what happened to him."

"No, worse—he does." Tim cleared his throat. "First, the letters on the wall weren't there when he went upstairs. We assumed as much, but now we've got confirmation."

"They were definitely a warning for me, then?" Ben asked.

"Unless the ghost opposes engineers on principle, I would say so." Tim shook his head. "When I asked Jared what happened, he swore a ghost pushed him down the stairs."

I almost fell out of my chair. "Excuse me?"

"My thoughts exactly. Says when he was inspecting the downstairs, the chandelier started shaking. It seemed unstable, so he went up. When he got to the apartment, he heard creaking, something moaned, and he got shoved. He rolled down the stairs and woke up in the hospital hours later."

"He didn't mention if the ghost was named Miles, did he?"

"Uh, I don't believe the spirit introduced himself," Tim said.

My head dropped into my hands. "This is miserable. How is Ben supposed to run a business when we have an angry ghost pushing people down stairs, flashing lights, and laughing like the bad guy in *Inspector Gadget?*"

"Can you bind the spirit?" Ben asked. "I, uh, have been watching reruns of *Ghost Hunters*."

"Only if I'm more powerful than he is. That's not a given. What if I bind him, Two Mules reopens, and the ghost bursts free when the place is full of patrons?"

"You're right," Ben said. "It's not worth the risk."

I turned to Tim. "What about the letters? Was it really blood?"

"The tests haven't come back yet. It could take about a week. The good news is, Jared isn't filing a police report. He doesn't want to testify to any of this. He's prepared to swear that he fell, which means, I can't tell you to stay out of the property. As long as the town is okay with you poking around, I won't try to stop you."

"I was planning to make the purchase after Jared completed his report," Ben said. "But I don't like any of this. If the ghost is attacking innocent people, I can't open to the public."

"You're right," I said with a sigh.

Ben asked, "Detective, are there any leads on who killed Miles?"

Tim shook his head. "We're still processing the evidence and trying to identify the people he was involved with back then."

Josie called through the door that dinner was ready, and

we all went to grab our plates. She'd made lasagna with garlic bread, two types of salad, and a mouth-watering tiramisu. Everything looked amazing. When we returned to the dining room with full plates, Walter sat at the table.

"I've been thinking about this, and maybe you're going about it all wrong," he said.

"Oh, yeah? What makes you say that?"

"I, uh, didn't say anything," Tim said.

Ben laughed. "She's talking to her grandfather. You'll get used to it."

My cheeks grew warm. "Sorry, I forget. He said we've been going about this all wrong."

"If you're going to repeat everything I say, this will take forever," Walter said. "Pink! Come in here, you silly cat!"

Before I could ask why, my cat bounded through the swinging door leading to the foyer and leaped onto the table.

"That's gotta be a health code violation," I said.

"Do you want my help or not?" he asked.

Ben's eyes widened. "Whoa."

"Did I hear what I think I heard?" Tim asked.

"Uh, depends. Did you hear a cat say, 'Do you want my help or not?' Pink makes himself understood by humans when he wants to."

Pink walked over to Tim and sat down, curling against his chest. "That's not my only trick." Then he stretched a paw toward Ben, who looked as confused as me. When my friend didn't move, Pink put his paw on Ben's arm.

Walter grinned. "Now that we all understand each other, let me recap."

Ben gasped. Tim managed not to make a sound, which probably came from years of performing interrogations, but his jaw clenched.

"Hold on. Did you guys hear that?" I looked at Pink. "Can you let them hear Walter?"

"You didn't know?" Ben asked. "I still can't see him, but I heard his voice."

I shook my head. If Pink could allow Walter to enter conversations with the living, that opened up a whole new world. I could stop translating when the cat was with us. After the promises needed to get him into my car, I wouldn't take him out much, but mansion life could be much improved.

"He sounds exactly like I remember," Tim said. "Hey, Walter. Long time. The town hasn't been the same since you passed."

"Aww, shucks, now you're making me blush. Listen, Miles isn't upset about being dead. Did you consider that he might be mad in general? Like, a cranky ghost?"

"A cranky ghost?" I sighed. "Do we think GhostCat's companion has the same abilities to manipulate objects? If not, how could a ghost push Jared?"

Pink said, "It depends on what he is. If both GhostCat and the other spirit are controlled by a talisman, yes."

"If someone were controlling him so the bar stayed empty, I'd expect them to come around and see what happened. We've been in and out all week, the police have dropped by twice, and Shady Grove is a small town. News travels fast."

"Fair enough," Tim said.

"Until we learn otherwise, the best way to proceed is to assume that Miles is trying to avenge his death. It's all we have to go on," I said.

"That's good, because investigating a human murder is the only way I can help," Tim said. He gestured around the table. "All this has me wondering if you might've slipped something into my food."

"Any leads?" I asked.

"A few. His parents are going to send me photographs. They also agreed to give DNA samples so we could confirm the man's identity. I left messages for a couple of other people. Sheriff Matthews wants to handle interrogations. I didn't have the heart to tell him he's chasing a ghost."

A friend of mine worked with Sheriff Matthews on a few cases. Her kindest assessment of him left me with zero confidence that he'd care about solving such an old case. But I had faith in Tim, and I was happy to let him explore the non-supernatural aspects of this case.

"What do you think?" I asked Pink.

"If the anger comes from the way Miles died, it should be abated when the police arrest his killer. However, it's been twenty years, so I wouldn't hinge everything on that."

"What if it's a talisman? Could I use it to force Miles to show himself to me?"

Pink considered me for a long time before nodding. "If the spells haven't been renewed recently, it's possible. You could also use it to find the witch who created it. Magic leaves traces, like a signature. Then you could—"

"Let the police question her," Tim interjected. "Right?"

"Absolutely," I lied.

That settled it. Tomorrow, I would find that talisman.

NINETEEN

The next morning, I meditated for almost an hour before leaving my room. I didn't know how big this talisman was, but I needed every bit of my power to locate it. Then I grabbed a quick breakfast and explained my plan to Ben. He had a meeting with the lawyer handling his stepfather's estate, so I started the search on my own. Well, on my own, with Walter. Although there wasn't anything for him to do except watch, he said he'd like to wander the candy store.

When I turned onto Second Street, movement around Two Mules caught my attention. Yesterday, the police department had replaced the old, tattered police tape surrounding the sidewalk with new stuff. It covered the door now, too. At first I thought that was what drew my eye, but the air was still. Something was moving inside the bar, and it shouldn't be.

Parked cars lined both sides of Second Street, as usual. Most of the owners would be in the coffee shop or one of the other stores. Ben wasn't meeting anyone today, though, and neither was I. Did the police come back to finish investigating?

I didn't see any police cars, so unless an officer drove their vehicle, no one should be in there. But how would someone get in? To my knowledge, only the town clerk's office had a key. Someone gave Ben a copy—did they do that for everyone? It seemed unlikely. Last night, the police officers left through the front door while Ben and I were still there. Had we engaged the locks behind them before leaving through the back? With everything going on, I couldn't swear to it. We might have inadvertently allowed someone an easy entry.

Instead of parking in the back lot as I'd intended, I turned into an alley that would let me avoid passing in front of the windows. If someone was inside the bar, I didn't want them to see me coming.

Maybe I was overreacting. It was possible that someone entered Cocoa Channel, or I'd spotted a reflection off the business across the street, but I didn't think so.

"Did you see that?" I asked, still looking for a parking space.

"You mean, did I see someone sneaking into Two Mules ahead of us?" Somewhere during the trip, my grandfather had changed into a Sherlock Holmes outfit, complete with a giant magnifying glass and pipe. "What do you think? Elementary, my dear Emma."

"You know, Sherlock Holmes never actually said—"

"Shush. Do I tell you how to role play?"

By the time I found a parking space, whoever I'd seen had been in the bar for at least five minutes. Although we'd never calculated the exact distance Walter could travel from me while using my necklace, I estimated it to be about a hundred yards. Not nearly enough for him to enter the bar without me and see who was in there.

We exited the car and inched down the sidewalk, my gaze never leaving the bar doors. When we stood in front of Grace's store, I paused. If anyone was inside Two Mules, this should be close enough to tell. "Can you go see who's in there?"

"Oh, sure! It's Grace and her assistant, and some shoppers. Ooh, that woman is getting chocolate covered Oreos! Excellent choice, ma'am."

Our mission forgotten, my grandfather moved into the sweet shop. I wanted to call him back, but there was no point. I might not be invisible, but I could check for intruders from right here.

Closing my eyes, I reached for my magic and sent it into the buildings, searching for any thread roughly ninety-eight point six degrees.

Grace had several customers forming a line from the front counter halfway to the door. Good for her. Even after tourist season ended, everyone loved candy. On the other side of Two Mules, I sensed Floyd's trademark jeans and chambray shirt with the sleeves rolled up. He was talking to someone, but my interest lay in the third business.

The main floor, as far as I could tell, was empty. My power found the faded velvet on the walls, but nothing else. I knew there were plenty of clothes in the basement, so next I checked the apartment.

According to my power, a medium-sized male walked around the upstairs. My breath caught in my throat.

Had Miles finally shown himself?

As my magic followed the thread's movement behind the closed blinds, my elation faded. Yes, someone was on the top floor of the bar. However, they were wearing clothes. Ghosts didn't wear clothes. Walter's clothes were purely decorative in the most literal sense—I couldn't sense them with my magic. Also, ghosts were cold.

This wasn't a ghost; it was a good old-fashioned burglar.

My first instinct was to reach for my phone, but I didn't want to be the out-of-towner who dialed 911 three times in less than a week.

Besides, everything else about this spirit flew in the face of my expectations. What if, somehow, he *was* wearing clothes? If I called the police *again* and no one was in there, I'd be a laughingstock.

Uncertainly, I hovered on the sidewalk while weighing my options. I could go in and confront the intruder, with no idea who they were, what they wanted, or if they were armed. I could get Walter and ask for his help. Or I could wait and see if anyone came out.

I tilted my head, listening for any signs coming out of Two Mules. Whoever went in there wasn't making any noise. Given all the reports of moaning and rattling chains over the years, that supported my burglar theory. The ghost had been loud.

As this person might be armed, I couldn't go racing in. Ben didn't need *two* ghosts haunting his new business.

A hinge creaked, making my decision for me. The door to Two Mules inched open. Whatever—whoever—went inside didn't want to be caught. Suddenly, neither did I.

My heart pounded. Before the intruder could exit the bar and find me lurking on the sidewalk, I dove through the door of Grace's shop.

Immediately, I cursed myself. Now there was no way to see who'd been in there! If I burst back out on the sidewalk now, the intruder would know I was onto them, and they might be dangerous.

The inside of Grace's shop was still bustling with activity. Several patrons lined up before the cash register, and four others waited at the order pickup sign. Grace stood behind the counter filling orders while a girl who looked about T's age ran the cash register. She looked up and met my eyes.

Walter stood pressed up against the glass display case, so close that if he needed to breathe, he'd be in trouble. There was no way to get his attention without alarming everyone.

Not knowing what else to do, I smiled at Grace. Then I sent a burst of magic through the windows toward whoever exited the bar. My power encountered a lanky form wearing blue jeans.

Teasing out a thread of magic, I hooked it to the belt loop of the person's jeans. This was like my locator spell, but allowed me to track a moving target. Hopefully.

It worked!

When I turned toward the exit, a thin pink thread stretched outside. Now I could follow at my leisure.

Bells above the doorway jingled as a large group left the sweet shop, and I slipped out behind them. If my quarry turned around, they would only see several satisfied shoppers leaving a candy store. When I got far enough away, Walter would be dragged along. I felt bad, but I had to follow my gut. Something told me identifying this intruder was important.

I scanned the street. No one was in sight, but my magic tugged me to the right, past Floyd's bait shop. Without hesitation, I followed the thread.

The person ahead of me seemed in no hurry, perhaps

wanting to blend in as much as I did. We walked down Second Street, then turned. I still couldn't see anyone, but trusted my magic to find a medium-height person wearing blue jeans and a flannel shirt for me. The only fabric on their feet appeared to be cotton. At first, that suggested I was looking for a person wandering the street in slippers. Then thunder cracked in the distance, and I realized: rain boots. Their plastic wouldn't register with my power.

Walter bounced into view. "I should refuse to speak to you for that."

"Sorry," I said sincerely. "Do you want to watch me eat a chunk of fudge later?"

"I can't tell if you're being extremely kind or cruel."

"You know I would feed you if I could. I promise I'll make it up to you. But right now, we're tracking someone who broke into the bar."

"Why didn't you say so?" Now that we had a mission, Walter was all smiles again.

After several minutes, the trail stopped at a nondescript office building. At first I thought they'd turned again, but the thread was now a dark pink, almost red, nearly half an inch thick.

Taking a deep breath, I threw the door open and followed. The thread disappeared at the elevator doors. Rather than check each floor as the metal box took me past, I headed for the stairs.

The thread continued to darken as it pulled me up one flight after another. On the fourth floor, however, it turned and pointed through the landing door into the lobby. My magic pulsed with the nearness of my target.

Pulling out my phone, I used the selfie cam to check my appearance. It wouldn't do to burst through the doors with wild eyes, yelling about magic threads. I took a deep breath and counted to ten. When my pulse returned to normal, I reminded myself this was a public building. If anyone asked what I was doing here, I could pretend to be looking for the taxidermist on the first floor. Pink might like a stuffed companion.

Finally, I steeled myself and opened the door, exiting into a hallway that contained the elevator bank. To my surprise, two men stood there.

Walter gasped. "Do you know who that is?"

The man facing me was unknown, yet still very familiar. His fiery red curls grew Einstein-style around his head, but he wore a neat button-up shirt with the sleeves rolled up and pressed black slacks. When he waved his hands to punctuate a point, I noticed black stains on his fingers.

A sign on the wall informed me I'd found the offices of the *Shady Grove Sentinel.* Einstein-hair spoke animatedly to his companion, whose back was to me. The sense of recognition grew stronger. The first man's outfit wasn't remotely like the clothing I'd sensed with my magic. But the other guy wore blue jeans, black rubber boots, and a flannel shirt. He had close-cropped red hair identical to the man opposite him, which left no question as to their identities.

The man skulking around the bar was none other than TJ Crews. The man who appeared right after Ben and I first saw the chandelier shaking, when we found Miles's body, and again after Jared fell.

TJ pushed Jared.

TWENTY

"I can't believe it," Walter said. "Why, I oughta wring his neck!"

I knew exactly how he felt. Nothing prepared me for this moment. TJ was a nuisance, but he'd never struck me as a criminal. Even when Tim said TJ exaggerated stories for the paper, somehow, I'd missed seeing his true self.

My first instinct was to run. Well, actually, my first instinct was to yell at TJ for causing so much trouble, but common sense quickly prevailed. Especially after Walter kicked him in the shins for me.

Before approaching, I took a deep breath and counted to ten, reminding myself I'd followed this trail for a reason. Running away would be counterproductive. We were in a public building, and I shouldn't be in danger from either of these men. Yes, they could be working together, but unless the elderly secretary visible through the glass doors was in on it, I should be relatively safe.

If I were wrong, well, I'd sew their clothes together and run away. Just in case, I texted my location to Ben and Josie.

But my power was strong, and after several days of struggling against something I couldn't see, part of me was itching for a good confrontation.

After gathering my courage, I dug for the righteous indignation I'd felt upon seeing TJ in the bar and stepped forward. "You! I should've known you were up to no good."

"Hello there!" the older man said. "I'm Hal Crews, editor. You must be here for the red-headed club meeting."

Self-consciously, I touched my ponytail. "There's a club?"

"I'm joking. Can I help you? This is my son, TJ, by the way."

"He's not joking," Walter said. "I used to be president of the club. But it's top secret. You need a reference."

"We've met," I said tightly to Hal. "Actually, that's why I'm here. TJ, what were you doing inside Two Mules about half an hour ago?"

He flushed. "I don't know what you're talking about."

"Oh no? Then why is there sawdust on your boots?"

TJ looked down and turned bright red. He started to speak, but his father intervened. "What is the meaning of this?"

"I'm sorry to bother you, sir. My friend wants to buy the old bar on Second Street. Your son has been causing problems since day one, and I want to know why. Did you push Jared down the stairs?"

TJ squeaked. His hands came up defensively. "What? No! Of course not!"

"Son, we've talked about this," Hal said sternly. "Did you trespass to get a story?"

"No one owns the building. It belongs to the town."

"Which means someone with authority needs to give

you the okay to enter," I said. "Ben had permission to scout. You didn't."

"Sounds like trespassing to me," Walter said.

"I don't have to tell you anything," TJ huffed.

"You're right, you can tell Sheriff Matthews." I pulled out my phone, but TJ stopped me.

"Okay, fine, I'll tell you. But not here."

"Let's go to my office," Hal said.

I hesitated, thinking of the advice to never allow a kidnapper to move you from one location to another. But this man once won an award for being an upstanding citizen, and I wanted to believe that counted for something.

"Hal's a good man," Walter said. "You'll be safe with him."

Emboldened by the recommendation, I followed.

The inside of the building reminded me of the set of *The Newsroom*, but on a much smaller scale. Other than the receptionist's desk at the front—Ethyl, according to her nameplate—there were only two desks. One was adorned with several large pictures of TJ, the other bare.

Hal saw where my eyes went. "That's for freelancers, if they come in. These days, almost everyone works from home, which might be why my son gets into so much trouble."

The editor-in-chief's office looked like a blizzard had passed through, dropping paper instead of snowflakes. He took a seat behind the desk and gestured for me and TJ to sit on the other side, but I preferred to stand. Once TJ plopped into the left-most chair, the other would leave him blocking my access to the door.

"Now, what is going on here?" Hal asked pleasantly. His gaze bored holes into his son's face.

TJ squirmed and covered his face with his hands. After a

moment, he dropped them and sat up. "I was trying to get evidence of the ghost."

A look of confusion crossed his father's face.

I simply asked, "Why?"

"It would sell a million papers. The AP would pick it up! I'd be a household name."

"More likely, you'd be offered a job with *The National Enquirer*," Hal said.

"Still better than this rag," he muttered.

"Oh, really? Better than getting paid to traipse around and harass people? Better than working for someone who lets you get away with everything? Boy, I've coddled you for too long."

"What was your plan, TJ?" I asked.

He pulled an electronic device out of his messenger bag. I'd seen similar ones online. "Electromagnetic recorder. There's also a trap, and a few other things."

Hal groaned. "Please tell me that's not why you asked for petty cash."

"It would've worked! I went in, set up the devices, took some pictures, adjusted a few knobs, then I recorded the desired results."

"*Desired* results, not actual? You mean you faked another story?!" Hal roared. He leaped to his feet and placed his hands on the desk, leaning forward. Then, as if realizing I was watching him, he glanced at me and took a deep breath. "We'll talk about this at home. Emma, are you satisfied with my son's confession? I assure you, he will never do anything like this again, even if I have to send him on assignment to Antarctica."

His words mollified me. Now that Hal was aware of the situation, I was no longer needed. There was just one thing to take care of before leaving.

I cleared my throat. "TJ, Ben is going to buy the bar in the next couple of days. Once he does, you are prohibited from setting foot on that property for any reason. If you do, we'll have you charged with trespassing. My lawyer will serve a formal notice next week."

"That won't be necessary," Hal said. "Will it, TJ?"

"No, sir," he mumbled, still not meeting my eyes.

"Now, apologize to Emma for scaring her. This is not the way we get stories."

He muttered the most insincere apology I'd ever heard, but I graciously accepted. I couldn't get out of the newspaper office fast enough. TJ had wasted our time since Ben and I first set foot in the bar, and I was over it.

Halfway to the door, something occurred to me. "How did you get in?"

"What?"

"The bar. I saw you enter through the front door, but it should've been locked."

"A magician never—"

"Answer the question," Hal said.

TJ avoided my gaze. "Lock picks."

Hal held his hand out silently. With cheeks that matched his flaming hair, TJ pulled several pieces of metal out of his pocket and dropped them into his father's waiting palm. "Again, Emma, I'm sorry."

After thanking Hal, I left, but not before asking the threads holding TJ's pants up to drop. The angry yell that followed brought a smile to my face, but a weight still hung around my neck. Eliminating a suspect should feel better. I could only wonder if Jared was telling the truth about being pushed by a ghost.

The situation bugged me the entire walk back to the bar. I still didn't trust TJ, but as obnoxious as he was, he was trying to sell newspapers. If he'd killed Miles, he'd stay as far away from the building as possible.

Also, he would've been about nine years old.

Theoretically, TJ could be covering for his father's crime, but that didn't fit. Hal was a pillar of the community; Walter said he was a great guy. The man had been named citizen of the year. Granted, it was by his own newspaper, which wasn't exactly an unbiased source, but still.

Pulling out my phone, I texted Aly.

> What can you tell me about Hal Crews?

> Hal's a great guy. No idea what happened to his son. When TJ printed a story that heavily implied I'm a killer, Hal was furious.

> I'm surprised TJ hasn't moved on yet. He always thought he was too good for us.

Her reply cemented it. Even if TJ had lied about why he was in the bar, I didn't see how he or his father could be involved in Miles's death. Between the Citizen's award, Walter, and Aly, I had to believe Hal was an okay guy.

Lucky was right: this bar was bad news. Maybe it wasn't meant to operate as a bar at all. Ben should walk away, and someone else could set up a nice cat cafe. Give GhostCat a special perch near the front windows. He'd like that.

But no matter how hard I tried, I couldn't let go. There must be a way to reclaim this space for the living, and I intended to find it. There was still the matter of that talisman. If it could be found and destroyed, GhostCat and Miles should leave the bar.

If a top-to-bottom search of the property revealed nothing, I would learn to perform an exorcism.

When I was halfway across the bar, the chandelier bulbs lit up. Though this had happened before, it never ceased to freak me out. As I watched, the entire fixture moved to the right, then the left.

Trying to sound brave, I called out, "Thanks, Miles! Now I can see!"

In response, the lights winked off.

"Hilarious! Listen, I'll be out of your hair in a few minutes, then you can go back to whatever ghosts do."

Again, the lights blazed. I'd thought they were bright before, but now the light seemed impossibly white, leaving streaks as the shaking intensified. Fear froze me in place.

This wasn't faulty wiring. This wasn't a friendly ghost like Walter or even GhostCat. If Miles had arrived, he wasn't happy to see me.

I stepped backward. The lights swung frantically overhead, making the shadows dance. Something pounded the ceiling above my head. Then another banging, this one somewhere in the walls.

The creaking above me grew louder. As I watched in horror, the chandelier detached itself from the ceiling and plummeted toward my head.

I screamed.

TWENTY-ONE

As the chandelier hurtled toward me, everything turned to slow motion. I couldn't move. Couldn't breathe. Every spell I knew flew out of my head. Walter shouted my name and dove behind the bar.

Then GhostCat jumped into my arms. Reflexively, I caught him.

Metal and glass pounded the ground, shattering. Closing my eyes, I braced myself, waiting to be bombarded with shards of glass and worse.

Nothing happened.

The silence was deafening.

A wet nose against my chin made me open my eyes.

GhostCat was still in my arms, nuzzling my face. We stood in a pinkish bubble, which shimmered in the air. When I touched it, lightning shot up my arm. Like static cling, yet oddly comforting. Pock marks covered the bubble.

It took longer than it should have to realize why. "Everything hit this bubble instead of us. You saved me?"

He nodded.

"Why?"

No response. Then he jumped down and trotted away. As he walked through the pinkish barrier, it vanished.

Walter stood. "Are you okay?"

"I think so. What happened?"

My legs shook. If the floor hadn't been covered with glass, I would've sunk to the ground. Instead, somehow, I made it to a bar stool before my knees buckled. Walter put his arm around me. Although I couldn't feel him, I rested my head where his shoulder should be. Somehow, it comforted me.

My mind whirled.

My first thought was that TJ had sabotaged the chandelier earlier. After all, I'd caught him red-handed, and he admitted wanting to fake a ghost sighting. But the timing didn't fit. Why rig the chandelier to fall an hour after he left? He couldn't have known when anyone would be here.

Could the accident have been a coincidence? I had a hard time buying it. Had Miles decided he didn't want us poking around anymore, or was it something else?

Before I could investigate, I needed to clean up the mess. It wasn't safe to walk around with this much broken glass on the floor. The broom was in the storage room off the kitchen, but that didn't matter to me.

With a deep breath to clear my mind, I reached for my hearth powers. In one big swoop, I pulled all the shards of glass toward me. There were about a billion.

Even with the electrical current turned off, I knew better than to touch the wires sticking out of the ceiling. I focused on the floor, using my magic as a broom, getting every tiny shard and a few remaining wisps of sawdust. There was a faster way, but the sweeping soothed me. By the time I finished, my legs had stopped trembling.

"This sure doesn't look like it did back in my day," Walter said, looking around at him.

"I thought you didn't come here."

"I had friends in Shady Grove. We came here once or twice before Leo took over. The chandelier is the same one they had in the early nineties, but the fabric on the wall was vibrant. The whole place was bustling then, full of energy. And we didn't have these weird light bulbs."

"What's weird about them? Are they little spirals?" Energy efficient bulbs weren't nearly as popular during my grandfather's day.

"No, there's a hole or something. Like someone cut a square in them. Look."

I hoisted myself off the stool, then waited to see if my knees held. After a deep breath, I went to the pile of debris and crouched down.

It didn't take long to see what Walter had spotted. With one catastrophe after another, we hadn't gotten close to a place where we'd need to replace any burned-out bulbs. I'd never paid much attention to the lights in the chandelier. Now, though...

I picked up the nearest intact bulb. As my grandfather said, there was a rectangular window on one side. Also a button on the top. Curious, I pushed it.

The light came on.

"Ack! A ghost!" Walter yelled, shielding his eyes.

"Ha ha," I said. "It's battery-operated. Who would put battery-operated bulbs in a wired light fixture?"

"Especially one hanging from the ceiling. You wouldn't be able to reach it."

He had me there. I flipped and turned the bulb in the beam of my phone's flashlight, looking for a manufacturer name or serial number. When I found it, it only took a moment to run a search from my browser.

It was a battery-operated, remote-controlled smart bulb.

"How would someone who died in 2002 know about light bulbs controlled by the internet?" I asked Walter. "Did you know they were a thing?"

He snorted. "I still don't know what they are, and I'm looking at one. The better question is, how would a ghost buy them?"

No ghost had a credit card or account at the local big box store, human or feline. Nor did a ghost possess a need for these things. A ghost also couldn't steal cash. But humans could, and humans did. Especially if a human wanted to convince people that a certain building was haunted to scare them away.

Ben and I had discovered the shaking chandelier on the day we arrived. Wi-Fi bulbs explained the flickering lights. They didn't explain how or why anyone would install such a thing, but it could have been part of TJ's master plan.

I went upstairs to see what other nasty surprises he'd left for us. The apartment looked the same as usual: massive windows, wall of bookcases, no furniture, hideous rug. Still, I paced the room, looking for anything out of the ordinary.

When I passed through the middle of the room, something creaked.

"Did you hear that?" Walter asked.

"Yeah." I cocked my head and listened, shifting my weight again. Another creak. "Just old floors, I think."

"Maybe, maybe not. You're right over the chandelier."

"You think it fell because the wood here is worn out?" I pushed the rug aside with my magic, noting how clean the floor was underneath. Then, getting on my knees, I ran my hands over the spot we'd identified. Hard and smooth, just like a wood floor. Curious, I knocked.

It echoed.

"Is that normal?" I asked.

"On the other side of this, there's a hole now, because the chandelier is gone. But you should still have some insulation or something, I'd think."

Not sure what I was listening for, I knocked again. This time I noticed something more interesting than the echo. The floorboard wiggled slightly around the nail holes. It was loose.

"You'll warn me if I'm about to fall through the ceiling, won't you?"

"Hold on, I'll check." Walter stuck his head through the planks before a muffled laugh came back. "You're going to want to see this!"

Without a hammer or nails, even a loose floorboard presented some challenges. I poked my fingernail in the crack and worked it for a minute. Nothing happened. Then I realized that the hole surrounding the nail appeared larger than necessary. Like the nails had been removed and replaced several times. I slid a fingernail under the metal and tugged. It slid out into my hand. Huh.

The other nails did the same until I swiveled the floorboard around to reveal the opening beneath. Did TJ do this? That supported my "TJ sabotaged the chandelier" theory.

Peering into the opening, I gasped to find a white cloth bag inside. Had TJ buried this? Or was Walter right all along, and someone hid Lucky's missing money in the bar?

When I picked it up, I realized the fabric wasn't a bag at it—someone had folded cloth around other items. They also had left an old tape recorder, what looked like a battery powered light, and a half-empty bottle of water. The battered tape recorder appeared to be far older than TJ, old enough that it made no sense for this to be his. The plastic bottle didn't have a speck of dust, suggesting it had been left here recently. When I set everything on the wooden planks beside me, I looked at the fabric cloth again. A white sheet.

Finally, I had my answers. This was the ghost of the Shady Grove bar. This was the thing Jared saw before getting pushed down the stairs. Not a supernatural spirit at all, just a human being with an agenda.

TWENTY-TWO

As I looked at the items stored under the floorboards in Lucky's old apartment, everything clicked into place. Miles's ghost couldn't manifest to the outside world. Maybe he couldn't manifest to me, either. Pink said it took a lot of energy.

Miles's ghost had never been the one driving people away. It was a real, living person. Someone with a vendetta against the bar, and probably the same person who killed him. All of which told me that, despite his many other flaws, TJ wasn't the one behind the haunting. It had to be someone else.

Someone, perhaps, who was displeased with drunk people wandering into his bait shop in the early hours of the morning and causing problems. But how would Floyd have gotten in? Surely the town wasn't full of talented lock picks.

The large windows facing the street opened approximately three inches at the top. No one was going in or out that way—even if a person could somehow ooze through the opening, it was a straight drop of twenty feet to the street.

The most obvious way in was the ancient fire escape leading from the parking lot below to the kitchen. The old lock appeared to be secure. When I attempted to open it manually, it stuck. After shoving with all my might didn't do anything, I reached for my magic.

When I'd first arrived at the mansion, I'd attempted a spell to remodel the exterior, something so far beyond my skill set at the time that the memory made me cringe. However, I'd learned a lot in the time since then.

In ancient times, witches made their own spell books, thick tomes frequently weighing many pounds. Three such grimoires were stored at the mansion: Walter's, his grandmother's, and my thin Lisa Frank notebook. Since lugging all three books around was out of the question, I'd brought my craft into the twenty-first century by retyping every spell, saving a searchable document to my hard drive, and sending a copy to my phone. Now I pulled my phone out and found Walter's remodeling spell.

Opening a window was much simpler than rebuilding an entire house. The incantation itself wasn't difficult. Closing my eyes, I recited the words and sent my power toward the wooden sill. With a mental shove, I pushed the frame as hard as possible. It crashed into the top of the opening. The building rattled.

Oops.

At least nothing broke.

After making sure the top wouldn't smash down on me, I poked my head through the opening. There was the staircase, exactly as I remembered. Thin metal steps that ended at least ten feet up. There was a ladder at the bottom you had to shove down to descend to the street.

Even though the window had resisted my efforts to open it, someone stronger might be able to do it without magic. I'd have to ask Ben to try the next time I saw him. Meanwhile, I wanted to see if this route was useable.

The metal shook when I put my weight on it. I closed my eyes, took a deep breath, and counted to ten. Then I asked my clothes to hold me up should I suddenly plummet. Hopefully, the spell wouldn't be needed.

"Are you sure about this?" Walter appeared beside me. "It doesn't look very sturdy."

"No, it doesn't."

"Why don't you let me go?"

"Because I'm trying to figure out how someone could break in and pretend to be a ghost. You don't need to break in."

Gingerly, I put my weight on the first step. It held. Then the second. After two-thirds of the way to the ground, the stairs ended at a pull-down ladder, as expected. I pushed on it. Nothing happened. I pulled, not expecting that to work. It didn't.

"Are you ready for me to say I-told-you-so?" Walter gazed down at me from the platform outside the window.

"No. You only get to say that if I fall and break my neck."

"You're stuck. No one can use the fire escape if the ladder doesn't work."

"It works, sort of. Hold that thought."

The metal ladder appeared to be rusted in place. Not terribly surprising, but it made it almost impossible that someone had used this window to enter the building.

Then I spotted the dumpster on the ground. It wasn't directly below me, but it was only a couple of feet off. The lid was closed. I should be able to jump onto it and scramble down from there. Someone taller than me could manage easily.

Okay, so our "ghost" was very agile, unlike me. That also made it more difficult to believe that sixty-year-old Floyd could be involved. He seemed to be in good health, but it was hard to imagine him climbing dumpsters and lunging for the fire escape. Grace, too. TJ could do it, and he was taller than me. He wouldn't have picked the locks if he could get in using the fire escape, though.

Rather than risk breaking a leg, I climbed back up the ladder.

"What do you think, Walter? How would someone get in here? Another window?"

"Not unless they fly."

He was right. If the person faking the ghost came in through the main floor, we would have seen them. There must be an entry point I hadn't noticed yet.

Standing, I surveyed the room while stretching out my back.

"Is there an attic?" Walter floated up, then right back down before answering his own question. "There is not."

"There's nothing," I said. "Unless they're climbing through the stove, it's the main door or one of the bookcases."

Although I'd expected him to chuckle at the notion of someone climbing through a bookcase, Walter tilted his head thoughtfully. "Didn't Lucky say there was a ghost in the bookcases?"

"No. She complained about being cold near them."

"Hold on." Walter disappeared through the wall. Five seconds later, he popped back through. "There's one on the other side, too. I bet it opens."

"Seriously?"

He crouched down, then pointed at the ground. "Take a look."

Crouching down, I peered at the wall until I found a tiny crack in a brick flush against the bookcase. Not a crack, a cut: it was an absolutely straight line, connecting with the floor at a right angle. It was too perfect to be a mistake. Following it with one finger, I stood, outlining a human-sized rectangle. "Brilliant, thank you!"

Walter beamed at me. "Told you. It was old Floyd all along."

I shook my head. "I should've known. I can't believe him! Come on."

"You aren't going to confront him, are you?"

"Of course I am! He's been faking a ghost for twenty years to put other people out of business."

"He also pushed someone down the stairs, and may have killed Miles. If Floyd is behind this, he's dangerous."

That gave me pause. Jared was about three inches taller than Floyd, more muscular, and probably at least twenty pounds heavier. Did Floyd get lucky with one big push? When I'd mentioned Jared's fall, he'd seemed distraught, but it could have been an act. What I'd interpreted as sadness and fear may have been guilt, or fear that Jared would wake up and identify him.

"I bet he was wearing the sheet," I said. "If he ran at Jared and waved his arms or moaned, that might have scared him down a step or two. Not sure how he planned to explain it if he got caught, though."

From this side, I didn't see an obvious way to open the hidden door, but I wasn't a hearth witch for nothing. The spell that opened the window should also work on this secret door.

"Will you check and make sure the room on the other

side is empty, please? I don't want to lose the element of surprise."

While Walter cased Floyd's apartment, I pulled the sheet over my head and adjusted it. The eyeholes didn't line up, but after a polite request to the fabric, they moved into the proper position. By the time I finished, he'd returned to give me the all-clear.

"Excellent." I beamed at him. "We're going to beat Floyd at his own game."

I could try pressing everywhere on the bookcase to look for a hidden latch. Or, I could resolve this now. One at a time, I called the bricks beside the bookcase to me before dropping them in a pile on the floor. Soon, I had a person-sized hole.

Walter clapped and floated ahead of me into Floyd's living room. "Oh, I wish he could hear me!"

"Me, too," I mumbled.

Walter went ahead to make sure Floyd was alone in his store. The last thing we needed was someone to spread rumors that the bar's ghost now visited the neighboring businesses.

As soon as he confirmed the coast was clear, I crept down the stairs. I didn't want Floyd to hear me until I was ready to reveal myself. My magic told me he stood behind the cash register, where he would see me open the door separating his apartment from the business. This had to happen fast.

I took a deep breath before raising one arm to point ominously ahead of me. Then I flung the door open and lowered my voice in my best impression of a ghost. "Floyd Fisher, I have a bone to pick with you."

Floyd jumped and spun around. When his eyes landed on me, he burst out laughing. "Nice try, Grace."

I whipped the sheet over my head. "Grace? You mean *Grace* is the ghost?"

His mouth fell open. The blood drained out of his face.

"Ooh, you've got him now!" Walter crowed.

Floyd pulled himself together. "Yeah. Um, Grace. Grace is the ghost."

It couldn't be more obvious that he was lying, if for no other reason than this sheet would drag on the ground if I weren't holding it up, and Grace was shorter than me. She wouldn't have made it two feet without tripping.

My eyes narrowed. "No, she's not. But she knows you are."

"I'm not saying anything else." He crossed his arms and glared at me.

"No problem. I'll play ghost. Looks like fun." The sheet trailed from my right hand. I dropped it, then sent my magic out to sweep up the fabric before it hit the ground.

With nothing attached, the sheet flew upwards, whizzing around the room in an arc. After completing the circle, it stopped in the air between us and twirled. Then, as if to punctuate my point, the sheet reached out as if there were arms underneath, waving the ends back and forth.

"Jazz hands!" Walter clapped. "I love a good jazz hand."

Floyd's eyes grew as big as saucers. "What are you doing?"

"Don't you know? The bar's haunted! I'm not doing anything. It's the ghost." Leaving the sheet hanging in the air, I moved around to the front of the counter and leaned forward, my eyes never leaving his. "Weird that the ghost needs a white sheet, though. Or Wi-Fi bulbs and a tape recorder."

His gaze darted to the door. He was closer than me, but I stood between him and it. He could race for the back exit, but he must have sensed I'd stop him. His shoulders sagged. "What do you want?"

"Why would you keep up this haunted bar charade for so long? What's in it for you? Operating next to an abandoned building can't be good for business."

"Better than the bar was," he said. "Listen, the whole thing started as a joke."

"You thought scaring Lucky away from her uncle's business was funny?"

"Not like that. A few weeks after Leo passed, I discovered the secret latch on the bookcase, purely by accident. Grace and I used it to explore the property. We avoided the bar when Leo ran it, so this was our chance to get a look. One night, someone saw our flashlights. We didn't know at the time, but the next day, we heard that someone had been in the building even though all the doors were locked. Grace made a joke. 'I bet it's haunted.' A few weeks later, some of Leo's friends were hanging around the sidewalk. I used the secret bookcase to go into the apartment and scare them away." He chuckled. "Man, the looks on their faces! That was great."

"I'm sure they were highly amused," I said, stone-faced.

"After that, the stories took on a life of their own. It was all in good fun. A private joke between me and Grace, and we didn't get along back then."

"Did she help?"

"In the beginning, yeah." He shook his head. "After about a year, she told me she was done. We'd had our fun, and she was ready to move on, hang out with people her own age. She agreed not to turn me in but vowed never to set foot in the place again. It was weird, almost like she found a new religion."

"Why did you keep the ghost thing going after Lucky took over?"

"The first time, we did it as a welcome, almost a rite of passage. Face the ghost and keep the bar! Of course, she didn't know that. And then... I don't know. It snowballed." Floyd sighed. "When Leo ran the bar, I'd have drunks sleeping in my doorway when I got here in the mornings. The whole sidewalk smelled like urine. It was disgusting. Every day, I'd have to clean up and shoo them away. I guess I thought a ghost might keep Lucky from following in her uncle's footsteps."

"Why not call the police back when it happened?"

"They didn't care. Leo paid them off. Heck, the old sheriff would sit in there, drinking everyone under the table. Then Lucky's new manager disappeared, and someone made a joke that Leo's ghost got him. That made me think—why not use the situation to my advantage? Things were better with the bar closed."

"You weren't worried about getting caught?"

"Oh, sure, but it was easy to make sure Lucky wasn't in the apartment before going through the bookcase." He winked at me. "Besides, the risk is part of what makes it so much fun."

I shook my head. "Lucky told me there was a draft that didn't come from the windows. She should've investigated."

"The opening is well-hidden," Floyd said. "I'm surprised you found it."

"Why did you push Jared down the stairs? I thought you were old friends."

Floyd chortled. "Oh, that's the best part! Jared did that. He thought it was hilarious. Got some fake blood, wrote the words, hid the container in the back of his truck, then took a couple of muscle relaxers and lay down to wait for you. We knew no one would search his vehicle. I wish I could've seen the look on that detective's face when Jared woke up and insisted a ghost pushed him."

I dropped the sheet. "Okay, fine. But things were going well. You didn't need an actual dead person to make the story work. Why did you kill Miles?"

"What are you talking about?" Floyd demanded. "I didn't kill nobody! Who's Miles?"

"Lucky's bar manager. The guy who disappeared."

"No one killed that guy; he ran away."

"We found a dead man in the basement, and we're pretty sure it's Miles," I said. "I'm sure you remember him."

Floyd said, "I barely knew that kid. He seemed okay. A bit fickle. You know, he was deeply in love with Lucky. They talked about getting married and everything. Then one day, out of the blue, he dumps her and starts telling me how Grace's eyes are the color of the sky and her smile lights up the world like the moon." He grimaced. "All kinds of poetic nonsense, but Grace seemed lonely, so I tried to be happy for them. Lord knows she needed more friends than the middle-aged curmudgeon down the block."

As Floyd talked, I searched his face for signs of dishonesty. He'd been so forthright about being the ghost, I believed he'd admit the killing, too, if he'd done it. Then the full meaning of his words sank in. Miles didn't just break up with Lucky. He dumped her for Grace.

"Grace?" Walter asked. "She never mentioned that."

"No, she didn't," I muttered, thinking. Then louder, "Lucky said he left her for someone else, but not who. I didn't think it mattered."

"Maybe she killed him," Floyd said.

"We explored that possibility. Are you sure Grace and Miles were dating and not friends, like she told me?"

"Oh, yeah. All moony-eyed. They'd come in here holding hands, like she was showing him off." He sighed and shook his head. "They say love changes you, but it didn't change Miles for the better. His entire personality transformed. Only ever talked about how amazing Grace was. Walked around like he was too in love to see straight."

"Sounds like he was in a trance," Walter said. "That's love spell stuff."

"Love spell?" I was so surprised, I barely cared that Floyd could hear me.

Luckily, he thought I was talking to him.

"Yeah, right. Grace gave him Love Potion Number Nine."

We needed to get back to the mansion to ask Pink about all this. I'd never suspected Grace possessed magic, but it wasn't like I declared my power to everyone I met. Besides, the magic store in Shady Grove was run by a witch who sold all kinds of ingredients commonly used in spells, including potions. Amira wouldn't sell the actual text—love spells made people dangerous—but someone who found the information could probably work it out. Even back around 2000, lots of stuff was online if you knew where to look.

"Uh-oh," Walter said, interrupting my thoughts. "Quick, hide!"

"What are you talking about?" I asked him.

"It's no use talking to the sheet," Floyd says. "I know there aren't any ghosts. Are you trying to convince me you're seeing things?"

Before I answered, the front door opened, and Grace

stepped inside. Quickly, I told the sheet to drop to the ground, hoping she hadn't seen it.

"Emma! What are you doing here?" she asked with a big smile.

"Oh, nothing. I dropped by to get to know Ben's new neighbor better. I was thinking about what you told me, how he petitioned to make this place a dry town."

Floyd let out a squawk. "What? I did no such thing!"

"Shut up, Floyd," Grace said. "I don't think the bar's ever going to reopen, do you? Not while it's haunted."

Warning bells went off in my head. This was dangerous territory. Something told me not to tell her Floyd confessed to faking the ghost. The less I let on about our conversation, the better.

I laughed nervously. "Yeah, you're right. The bar is definitely haunted. It's time for us to move on. It was nice seeing you!"

"Nice try," she said. "I know Floyd told you everything. I've got a listening spell on this place, in case the old man ever turned on me."

She stepped further into the room. The deadbolt clicked into place, then she flipped the sign on the door to "Closed" and dropped the blinds. "We should talk about this a bit more. Would you like to come upstairs and have some tea?"

"The gig's up, Grace," Floyd said. "I already told her about the ghost. Would you believe she thinks we killed someone?"

Grace turned toward him and raised a gun I hadn't noticed tucked against her side. "Yes, I believe it."

Before I could react, she fired.

TWENTY-THREE

The gun exploded. Floyd screamed. Instinctively, I lurched toward him. He dropped behind the counter, below my line of sight. A burst of magic escaped me, but I didn't even know what it did.

"Freeze." Grace turned her attention my way.

My hands went up. "I just want to see if he's okay."

"I'll check him," Walter said.

"Don't move," Grace ordered. To my surprise, she wasn't looking at me. "I may not be able to shoot you, but I can shoot her."

My jaw dropped. "You see Walter?"

"You see me?" he asked. "How do I look?"

"Yes, I can. I also hear him, and I know you can as well. I don't know if he communicates with anyone else, but it's a risk I can't take. Sorry, Grandpa, it's time for you to move on."

She raised the hand not holding the gun and pointed it at Walter. I didn't know what she planned to do, and I wasn't going to wait to find out. As she recited an incantation, I silently asked the thick cord holding my locket to open.

The knot in the thread untied itself. In the same instant, Grace finished her spell. Walter vanished. So did the necklace.

I couldn't be sure whether they went to our home or the Great Beyond. It seemed like the necklace opened up before she finished her spell, but Grace looked satisfied. Then again, she didn't know what I'd tried to do. She couldn't suspect I might have thwarted her.

I let out a wail. "How could you? Walter is harmless! He would never have said a word."

"No, but what if he follows me around after you're gone? I can't take that chance again." She shuddered.

"Again? You had a ghost before?" It all clicked into place. "GhostCat. But if you know this place is haunted, why fake a ghost?"

"Why do you think I stopped? I can't even enter the property now. That infernal cat knows I needed to get inside, move Miles's body where it wouldn't be found, and he wouldn't let me in!" She sighed. "Twenty years I've been trying to get past that beast's protection spells, and you did it in three days. How?"

"I think he liked Walter," I lied. "Why did he let Floyd in?"

"Floyd's harmless. GhostCat sensed your power the moment you got out of the car. He couldn't know if you were working with me or not, but he refused to take that chance."

Floyd was silent behind the counter, which made me fear he hadn't survived the shot. If she'd grazed him, I'd have heard *something*.

With a silent prayer, I reached for the threads of his

shirt and ask them about holes or blood in the fabric. Nothing. Did she hit his face?

Then I realized his cotton t-shirt rose and fell steadily. At the moment, Floyd was alive. Hopefully, he'd stay that way.

I also needed to keep Grace's attention on me. If she realized her first shot hadn't killed him, she might finish the job. Better to keep her talking.

"What did you do to my grandfather?" I demanded, hands on my hips.

"No biggie. Just a little spell to help him move into the afterlife." She waved one hand. "A way of saving humans from malicious spirits."

"What are you? Witch, medium?"

"Oh, no. I'm the one with the gun. You first, sweetheart."

I resisted the urge to roll my eyes at her. "I'm a hearth witch. Seeing ghosts is one of my powers, although I don't think all hearth witches do it. I would have guessed you're a medium until you threw magic at Walter. I've never seen anything like it. Your turn."

"I should've guessed hearth witch," she said derisively. "Anyone else would have attacked by now, but what are you going to do, clean me until I hand over the gun?"

"My powers aren't suited for battle," I lied. I couldn't shoot lasers out of my eyeballs or inflict direct injury, but the ability to manipulate someone's clothes had helped me before. Those people didn't have their pointer fingers wrapped around a trigger, though. I had more confidence in talking my way out of this—or distracting her until someone showed up—than trying to use my magic faster than she could shoot me. "Would you like me to wash your dishes?"

Grace snorted. "It's too bad we didn't meet earlier. We probably could have been friends under other circumstances."

"What happened?" I asked, desperate to keep her talking. "Why would you kill Miles? Lucky said you were friends."

"I already know Floyd told you about my relationship with Miles, so there's no use playing dumb." She motioned with the gun toward the open back door. "We're a little exposed here. Let's head somewhere more private."

Although conventional wisdom said never to leave with a kidnapper, I wanted to get Grace away from Floyd. Besides, if she slipped on the stairs, even a little, I might be able to use my magic to save myself.

My best shot at getting her to drop the gun was to tie her sleeves together, but with a gun pointed at my head, I wasn't desperate to try it. She'd get a shot off before it became impossible. Something needed to distract her enough to point the gun somewhere else, even briefly.

At her direction, I inched back up the stairs into Floyd's apartment. I briefly debated pretending to fall on her, but that wouldn't end well. Grace followed, the gun never wavering. She had the steadiest hands I'd ever seen. She was going to kill me.

No, I shouldn't think that way. Walter returned to the mansion. He would help if I stalled long enough. "What did you have against the bar? I'd think drunk people would be more willing to buy candy. Honestly, you had me convinced Floyd was the one behind all this."

She snorted. "He'd never have the nerve. At one point I considered trying to talk him into going to the basement and taking care of Miles for me, but he probably would have fainted."

"Were you behind Leo's divorce, too?"

"Oh, no. I wish I could take credit for that, but naw. I liked Old Leo. He was nice to me. So was his wife, for the most part."

"What did you have against Lucky? I thought her boyfriend dumped her for you. Sounds to me like you won. Why kill him?" Then Floyd's earlier words came back to me. "Did you put a love spell on him?"

"You're too smart for your own good," she said bitterly. "If it helps at all, I loved him."

"Not really."

"Well, aren't you perfect? I grew up with Miles, loved him my whole life. When he told me he planned to propose to Lucky, I panicked and found a spell to make him love me instead. It worked at first, but the spell needed to be renewed. Eventually, he found out. He was going to tell Lucky everything. I couldn't..." She took a deep breath. "If he'd told people what I did, I'd have lost everything. They burn witches at the stake, you know."

"Not around here, they don't," I muttered.

"I didn't want to kill him, but I didn't have a choice."

"You always have a choice."

"Unbelievably, things got worse. After Miles died, he followed me around, taunting me. I was miserable."

"Couldn't you make him go away, like you did with Walter?" I waggled my fingers at her. "Send him to the afterlife?"

A mirthless laugh escaped her. "You'd think so. That was the plan, actually. But no, GhostCat got in my way."

"I don't understand."

"Cat was my familiar. He lived with me, helped me, taught me. We were a team. Then he turned on me. When

Cat found out I'd done a love spell, he was furious. He's the one who told Miles the truth."

"Hold on. You named your cat 'Cat,' he died, and now he's GhostCat?"

She narrowed her eyes. "Don't you have a familiar? You should know, you can't name them unless they let you. Cat was very by-the-book. He was a cat, so he asked me to call him Cat."

"You didn't kill him, too, did you?"

"No. This all happened twenty years ago. He was protecting Miles until he passed, then his ghost took over. I still can't believe he let you in the bar." She turned toward the wall between the buildings and yelled, "Traitor!"

"When you say he's protecting Miles, you mean he's stopping you from moving the body?"

"Yeah, but it's more than that. After he died, Miles haunted me for weeks. Everywhere I went, he followed. I tried to leave town, but he came with me. I couldn't get any peace."

"Why haven't I seen him?"

"I made a talisman to suppress his spirit. Nothing takes care of Cat, though."

"So where is Miles?"

She shrugged. "Somewhere like purgatory, I guess. A kind of waiting room between the worlds."

How awful. Twenty years spent waiting for something to happen. If I got out of here alive, I needed to find the talisman so Miles could go free.

"If GhostCat banished you from the bar, why didn't you leave town? Move away from Shady Grove and never look back?"

She sighed. "I can't. Can't even take a vacation. It's part of the curse. I'm stuck here, worrying someone would uncover Miles's body and link it to me. Then you came along, and here we are."

We'd been talking for a while. Walter should have told Pink what happened, and he would have gotten Josie to call the police. Willow Falls was half an hour away, but the Shady Grove police could be here in a matter of minutes. Unless...

I swallowed, forcing that thought out of my head. I couldn't stand the idea of Walter being banished to the afterlife without so much as a goodbye. He had to be at the mansion.

Grace kept the weapon pointed at my face this entire time. I needed a distraction. If no aid was coming, I'd have to create my own. Unfortunately, we stood on highly polished hardwood floors, so there was no pulling the rug out from under her.

"That's enough talking, don't you think? I've got to make it look like the ghost got you, too." She cocked the gun, and her smile widened. "There are some weird rumors about you. Let the townspeople think you wanted to be a ghost."

Her words sent a wave of terror through me.

"You don't have to do this," I said.

"True. But I kind of want to. Isn't that something?"

Beyond the bookcase, I heard pounding. The police were here! I'd never been so relieved in my life.

"Oh, no. No way." Grace turned the gun as she yelled through the still-open doorway. "You come in, and this girl is dead."

For a split second, her attention wavered. I grabbed the opening. Calling on my magic, I asked the threads in her sweater to yank her arms straight up. Then I clapped, bringing her arms together. She still held the gun, but now she could only point it at the ceiling. The threads in her sleeves grew, winding around her wrists until not even a hair could fit between them. Grace screamed. A shot fired. Plaster rained around me.

"Emma!" someone yelled my name from below.

"What are you doing to me?" Grace screeched.

Feet thundered up the stairs. Based on the noise, I expected the officers to come in through the bookcase opening, but they must have surrounded the building.

"In here," I called. "I'm okay."

Relief flooded through my veins. Walter saved me.

TWENTY-FOUR

Tim barreled through the doorway, only pausing briefly when he realized Grace's arms were sewn together over her head. After he took her gun, he attempted to lower her arms, but they were stuck. "You're okay. What about her?"

"Sorry." With a snap of my fingers, I took the magic back. Tim blinked several times, but it wasn't his first encounter with my powers.

By the time he finished cuffing Grace, Sheriff Matthews arrived. "The rest of the building is clear. I'll take her."

Tim released her and came to me in two long strides. His eyes moved from the top of my head to the tips of my toes and back before he seemed satisfied that I wasn't injured. "How are you? I know you can take care of yourself, but..."

"I'm fine, thanks to you."

"What do you mean? You had the whole thing sewn up by the time I got here. Pun intended."

"If you hadn't provided a distraction at the key

moment, I couldn't have stopped Grace. She was clutching the gun too tightly for me to risk a spell without her firing."

"What do you mean? I just arrived."

My brow furrowed. "Before you came in, you banged on the wall, didn't you? That's what made her turn away from me, and I seized the moment."

Tim shook his head. "We heard the pounding when we arrived. It sounded... I was so scared she threw you down the stairs like Jared."

"Then what was it?" I turned toward Lucky's old apartment. GhostCat sat in the hole I'd left in the wall, wearing an expression suspiciously like a smile. Going over, I crouched. "Thanks for saving my life."

GhostCat let out a purr before flopping down on his back and exposing his furry stomach. Leaning forward, I rubbed his belly before turning back to Tim. "Turns out, the bar has a ghost, after all. And he's a good boy."

Behind me, Grace cursed at the poor kitty.

"Careful with her," I said when Sheriff Matthews led Grace toward the stairs. "She's, uh, got some special abilities."

"Special like you?" He raised an eyebrow. "I've been sheriff of this weird little county a long time."

"Still, you should call someone from the Magical Enforcement Office to bind her," I said. "I can't do it."

Grace smirked. "I'd love to see you try."

"What about me?" Another voice interrupted as a cloud of smoke filled the room. When it cleared, Dottie stood in the middle. I'd never been so happy to see my mentor.

"That's quite an entrance," I said. "What about being discrete?"

"Everyone here is in on the secret."

"The sheriff knows?" That was news to me. Aly encountered Sheriff Matthews all the time, and she never even hinted that he knew about her powers. Then again, they didn't get along.

"Of course he does. With all the magic in this town, sometimes our agencies need to work together. Now hold on while I take care of this." She gestured at Grace, who had turned pale. Dottie muttered a few words under her breath and waved her hands before giving a thumbs up to the sheriff. He shook his head, then he and Tim took Grace downstairs.

"I'll be back," Tim mouthed over Grace's head. I smiled at him before turning to my mentor.

"How did you know? What are you doing here? Not that I'm not happy to see you."

"The sheriff has a spell to summon me. Looks like an AirTag, fits in his pocket. He can activate it any time."

"Can you help me with one more thing? Grace said she made a talisman to banish the man she killed from this plane. I'd like to destroy it so he and GhostCat can move on."

"I'm happy to. It's probably in her apartment. We should check before the police search it for clues."

"We should also do it before Tim comes back and tells us not to."

With the help of a spell Dottie flat-out refused to ever teach me, we slipped down the stairs and out the front door. An ambulance and two police cars were parked in front, the flashing lights still pulsing. Grace fumed in the back of the police car.

I was relieved to see a paramedic talking to Floyd while loading him and a stretcher into an ambulance. Since Dottie had frozen everyone, it was impossible to hear what they'd been saying, but Floyd's eyes were open, and his expression indicated he was an active participant in their conversation. Floyd was going to be fine. Immediately, my heart grew lighter. While I wasn't responsible for Grace's actions, I'd never forgive myself if my impulsive decision to confront the older man got him killed.

Dottie tugged on my arm, drawing me through Cocoa Channel and up the back stairs to Grace's private apartment.

Whatever I expected a murderer's bedroom to look like, this wasn't it. Grace had decorated in bright yellow, with a beautiful sun rising over a flowerbed painted on one wall.

A large, sheet-covered dresser filled most of the opposite wall. On top of the sheet, someone had laid out candles, incense—and a small sachet shaped like a heart. Remembering what Pink said, I probed it with my power.

The threads holding it together definitely contained magic. Not the same as mine, but similar enough.

From the door, I pointed. "There it is, but I'm not touching it."

"A wise choice. We need to neutralize it. Let me do a binding spell, then we'll pull the pieces apart, separate them, and burn them." She said a few words. A bright light flashed on the talisman, then faded away. "Now we need scissors."

"Not so fast," I said.

The talisman was four inches wide and made of felt. Two pieces sewn together with something in the middle. With my magic, I asked the threads to release. The sides fell apart, revealing a dried-up lump of herbs on top of a small photograph. I couldn't see it from here but assumed it must have been Miles.

"Nice trick," Dottie said.

Movement drew my attention to the floor, where

GhostCat rubbed against my ankles. Leaning down, I scratched him behind the ears. "You're welcome."

An enormous yawn brought me upright. A man now stood in the corner, stretching and rubbing his eyes. He looked exactly like the newspaper image of Miles, and the painted wall was plainly visible through his body. "Wow, I've been asleep—who are you?"

"I'm Emma, and this is Dottie," I said, looking the man up and down. He was in his mid-twenties, with dark brown hair and kind eyes. "You must be Miles."

He nodded.

Dottie said, "Hold on. You see him?"

"You can't?"

"No, I see the cat, but that's it. I don't normally see ghosts, though."

"He's here. I'll translate," I said. "Miles, what happened? Why did Grace kill you?"

Miles said, "We grew up together. We were friends for a long time, starting in kindergarten. When I was twenty-one, I realized she had feelings for me, but I wasn't interested. Then I met Lucky, and the two of us hit it off immediately. Love at first sight. Grace never liked Lucky, but she acted happy for me until I told her I planned to ask Lucky to marry me."

"Let me guess, she didn't take it well?" I asked.

"She freaked out. Screamed, raged, threw things, insisted I leave her house immediately. About halfway home, I started feeling weird. The next morning, I woke up full of this intense love for *Grace*. I didn't know where it came from. My mouth was saying things, and my body was moving, but my brain had detached. Everything got hazy after that. One night, I don't know how much later, I woke up, and the cat was lying beside me. He did something...I can't explain it, but it was like he lifted a veil that had been over my eyes. Then he spoke."

"Did you freak out?" I remembered learning Pink could talk.

"I thought someone slipped me drugs. When I calmed down, he explained everything."

"A love spell," Dottie said knowingly, once I'd repeated his explanation.

"Yeah. I confronted her. She confessed, swore she didn't want to hurt me, but she loved me too much to let me marry someone else. I told her Lucky and I were going to be together, and I never wanted to see her again. I'd have begged Lucky to sell the bar and move away. That's how much Grace scared me."

"But you never got the chance," I said. "She killed you."

"Killed me, stole the bar's money, and made it look like I abandoned my love. But I didn't go away. I stayed here. At first, I followed Grace around, trying to get her to confess. I went to Lucky, but there was no way to communicate. No one heard me except the woman who killed me." He sighed. "Eventually, I resigned myself to having to spend my life with Grace after all, but I didn't have to like it. I taunted her. I practiced interacting with people, trying to tell them what she did. Cat took my side, protecting me from her. When he became a ghost, she made the talisman to banish me."

"How did he die? I thought familiars lived for ages," I said.

Miles nodded. "Their natural life span is long, but they're not invulnerable. After Grace killed me, GhostCat became very sick. Another witch took him to a vet, but they couldn't find anything wrong. It was like her evil poisoned him."

"That's terrible," I said. "You mean, if I do bad things, it affects Pink?"

"He certainly wants you to think so," Dottie said.

"Here I thought he was helping me out of the goodness of his heart," I muttered.

"Maybe he is," Miles replied. "But don't test it by killing people."

"I'll do my best," I said wryly before returning to our prior discussion. "This whole time, you were trapped here, watching, in between worlds? That sounds awful."

He shrugged. "Time is different when you're dead. It wasn't fun, but I believed, eventually, someone would set me free. And here you are."

"Here I am. Do you think you can move on now that Grace has been arrested?"

"I hope so. Will you give Lucky a message for me?"

The words warmed my heart. If their love transcended his death, anything was possible. Maybe a cop could even love a witch who kept messing up his investigations. "I'd be honored to."

Miles recited the message as Tim's footsteps announced he was coming upstairs. He cleared his throat when he arrived. "We're going to need a crew in here to process the crime scene, and you two shouldn't be here. Emma, I feel like I'm saying this a lot: I need to get a statement."

"That's my cue," Dottie said. "I assume no one wants to put my role in any of this into writing."

Tim smiled at her. "Couldn't explain you if I tried."

"Thanks, again," I said.

"Happy to help." She winked. "You'll make it up to me."

"Bye!" Miles called. "Nice to meet you, even though you can't hear me."

I relayed the message, and Dottie blew a kiss toward

Miles's corner before vanishing. I sighed wistfully. As much as I loved my car, I really wished I could teleport.

Tim looked from the empty wall to me and back. "Is your grandfather back?"

"No, that's Miles," I said. "The man in the barrel."

"Good. I'd feel weird doing this in front of your grandfather," he said. "Are you really okay?"

"I am. She didn't hurt me, but I need to check on Walter."

He ran his hands down my arms as if needing to see for himself. His brown eyes were filled with concern. When he got to my waist, he picked me up. "Checking on Walter can wait another minute, can't it?"

Grinning, I brought my arms up around his neck. "I think so."

When he kissed me, it was more than worth the wait.

TWENTY-FIVE

After I convinced Tim I'd live to sew another day, I called Josie. She confirmed that Pink had her alert the police when Walter returned to the mansion. According to my cat, Walter was fine but tired. The jump home wore him out.

"Can I talk to him on the phone?"

"Good question," Josie said. "Can you?"

I thought for a minute. "Maybe on speaker? But you don't know where he is. Never mind. I'll find him when I get home. I hope he feels better by then."

"Pink thinks he'll be fine. Do whatever you need to do and don't worry about us."

After our call ended, I turned to Miles. "Are you ready?"

He moved in front of the mirror, still holding GhostCat, and peered intently at the lack of reflection. "How's my hair? I can't see my hair!"

"It looks great," I said honestly. "Also, I think GhostCat should stay here. It'll freak Lucky out if she sees him and not you carrying him."

"Good point."

The drive to Lucky's house only took a few minutes. After I rang the bell, her voice came from the small rectangular box.

"Hold on. I'll be right there."

Miles jumped and looked all around the porch. "What? Where? How?"

I pointed at the device. "There's a speaker in the doorbell. The technological advances since you passed away are incredible."

"Considering how much your car resembles a spaceship, I believe it." He sighed. "Too bad I never got to see the world transform."

Lucky answered the door, taking away the need for me to respond. "Come in, come in. I was baking cookies. You can be my taste tester."

As I followed her into the kitchen, she talked about her new recipe, how she'd been working on finding herself since our last visit, and how she was trying to move on. "I even signed up for a dating app! Imagine that. Me, swiping right. Or left. Or whichever one means I like someone."

Miles looked so crestfallen I wanted to hug him. Instead, I cleared my throat. "Speaking of, there's something I have to tell you. We solved the mystery of the ghost at the bar."

"Was it Floyd? Years ago, I told everyone it was probably Floyd, trying to stop drunk people from hanging out by his bait shop in the early morning hours." She paused. "Come to think of it, that might be why he doesn't like me."

A snort escaped me. "Actually, yes, but that's not the whole story. Miles didn't run away. He was in love with you, and he wanted you. Grace tried to force him to be with her, and when it didn't work, she killed him."

Lucky's eyes grew wider with each word. When I

finished, she swallowed. A long moment passed before she spoke. Her voice cracked. "Are you sure? Did she tell you that?"

I glanced at Miles. He'd asked me to deliver a message, and I would, but he preferred she didn't know he was here. The information wouldn't bring her peace. He nodded as if to encourage me.

"I'm sure," I said. "Grace told me Miles swore he would never love her, that you were the only one for him, and he was going to propose. She killed him, then encouraged Floyd to keep faking the ghost so the bar stayed closed. She didn't want anyone to find Miles's body. Floyd didn't know what she'd done, so he agreed."

"How did you get her to tell you this?" Lucky asked suspiciously.

"She lied to me and Ben about her relationship with Miles. Floyd told me the truth. Once I confronted her, I think she wanted to brag about getting away with it for so long. She seemed proud of herself." I paused. "She's being taken to the police station."

Lucky shook her head. "I was so stupid. If only I'd listened. Miles told me we should move away, start a new life somewhere else. This is all my fault."

"No, it's not," he said.

"He doesn't blame you," I told her. "Grace is the only one at fault here. Miles wants—would want, I mean—you to be happy. To find love again. Don't waste your life beating yourself up or wishing he were still here."

She sighed. "I wish I could tell him how much I loved him one last time."

Behind her, Miles smiled.

"He knew," I said. "And he loved you, too."

As if to highlight my words, a mahogany wood-paneled

door shimmered into view beside Miles. The top was rounded, and a heavy gold knocker sat on the front. It was beautiful, practical, and timeless.

He turned toward the entrance, and the door swung open. From this angle, I couldn't see what lay on the other side, but his face lit up. When he looked at me, he radiated joy and peace. "Thank you, Emma, for this moment."

"Thanks," Lucky said. "I know you're trying to make me feel better, but it feels true. I appreciate you."

"It's my pleasure," I told them both honestly. "I hope you can be at peace now."

EPILOGUE

The old Two Mules was barely recognizable in the new, improved Raise Your Spirits. With my ability to move furniture magically, it took less time than expected to get the bar ready. By early December, my Shady Grove friends and I gathered to witness the opening.

Ben leaned into the "haunted bar" theme, and I loved the results. The walls had been transformed to depict a graveyard, complete with ghosts peeking out from behind headstones. Dim lighting and fake smoke brought a spooky glow to the scene. Sheeted figures hung from the ceiling. Every hour or two, the lights flickered, and a moan sounded from speakers hidden in the ceiling. Ben even strategically placed remote-controlled fans to send a chill through the air sporadically.

GhostCat roamed the gleaming countertop, looking for hands to pet him. Ben worried he might be a health code violation, but as fluffy as GhostCat looked, he didn't have actual fur. He didn't shed, but he could prance and preen under the customers' admiration. Most people thought the not-quite-real animal was a trick, but no one except me knew how Ben pulled it off.

My friends and I had requisitioned a large table, where I sat sandwiched between Aly Reynolds and the man I was now happy to call my boyfriend. On the other side of the table, Olive and her wife, Maria, sat with Amira, the owner of the magic shop. We were probably the only table in this place without an alcoholic beverage on it, but alcohol could do strange things to magical powers.

"What do you think?" Maria asked me. "Real or fake ghosts?"

"Ben's secret dies with me," I said, crossing my heart elaborately.

Tim grinned at me. "Just promise it will be a very long time before that happens."

I shivered and leaned into him. He put his arm around my shoulders. "I'll do my best."

"Now that the bar is finally open, what's your next project?" Tim asked.

"Well, first, I'm hoping for a quiet holiday season. Christmas is coming up fast. We're going to go to New York City to see the tree in Rockefeller Center, scout out the best lights—Walter wants to hire a designer for the mansion. He's got free rein, as long as he explains his vision well enough for me to write it down coherently."

"That should be fun. When I was a kid, the mansion hosted massive Christmas parties every year. My parents loved them."

I smiled up at him. "I'm really excited."

"Can't wait to see the finished display."

Across the table, Olive looked up abruptly. Her mouth dropped. "Never thought I'd live to see the day."

Amira gasped. "Nick!"

"What's wrong?" Aly asked.

Instead of replying, Olive stood up and beckoned. A stocky man with short salt-and-pepper hair, brown eyes, and an incredulous expression approached. When he turned toward us, I noticed a strong resemblance to Amira and a deep wariness in her eyes.

"This is Nick," she told us.

"Amira's brother," he proclaimed.

"You have a brother?" Aly asked.

"Half-brother," Amira hissed, so quietly I barely heard her. "He moved away forever ago."

"I had to see what they did with my old bar," he said, shaking his head. "Wouldn't let me sell it as non-haunted, and here we are."

Olive introduced the rest of us. When she got to me, I said, "I've read a lot about you."

"All good, I hope." He laughed loudly and poked Amira, who scowled. "You must not have been talking to my family."

"Well, you've been gone almost fifteen years," Amira said pointedly. "Right after you brought shame on us."

"You know you missed me, sis." Nick planted a kiss on her head before addressing the whole table. "I'm moving back to town! Got a job teaching at Maloney College next semester. This is a scouting trip, to find a house nearby. Can't stay with my sister forever."

"Can't stay with your sister now," she said with a deceptively pleasant smile.

He grunted.

"Maloney College?" Aly asked. "I'm a student there. What do you teach?"

"Drama, of course." He threw his arms out. "Who but a

fine thespian could have made everyone believe this was a truly haunted bar?"

"Just about anyone," Tim muttered under his breath. I suppressed a smile.

"You're admitting you conned people," Maria said.

"Don't be ridiculous. I put on a good show, and that's what I promised. Speaking of a good show, can I count on you to audition for the play, Aly? It's going to be something special."

She hesitated. "I'm not much of an actor. My major is biology."

"Don't say that. We're all actors! Think about it. When was the last time you lied about something?"

Aly's cheeks turned bright pink. Olive coughed, and I suddenly became very interested in my coffee.

"My daughter goes to school with Aly," Tim said. "I'll ask her if she's interested."

"Excellent!" Nick glanced at the bar. "Now, if you'll excuse me, I have to speak with the new owner."

When he left, I elbowed Aly. "What do you say? Want to become Shady Grove's next big thing?"

She glanced at Tim over my head. "I'm happy to watch Tiffaneigh from the sidelines. But I don't mind helping with sets and stuff."

"Either way, it'll be an experience."

Emma's friends will be back soon. What happens when disaster strikes the college play? Find out in the next Shady Grove Psychic Mystery, The Psychic's the Thing

AUTHOR'S NOTE

I'm sure some of you rolled your eyes when Grace told Emma the bar is "legally haunted." It's only almost as ridiculous as it sounds. That anecdote was taken from a Stambosky v. Ackley, a New York Court of Appeals case from 1991. It's an interesting read.

While indie writing seems like a solo activity, it takes a village. I couldn't do this without the online support of my writing team: the individuals who give feedback, the writer groups that are always generous with their advice, my amazing cover designer (seriously—it's like she creates what's in my heart), my fantastic editor—who keeps better notes on my plots and characters than I do, and everyone else who contributed to bringing this series to life. At the same time, an enormous thank you to my friends who let me lean on them for support, whether they know anything about the writing world or not, the ones who offer to proofread for typos, and of course, my amazing husband. None of this would be possible without his love and support.

I hope you enjoyed Emma's story. She's such a fun character, and I've loved being able to dip my toes into her world. I hope to return before too much time passes. The Haunted Haven series is a spin-off of the Shady Grove Psychic Mystery series, which follows Aly Reynolds as she discovers and learns to manage her psychic powers. Olive is a huge presence in that book. and Tim's daughter Tiffaneigh has a recurring role. If you haven't read Aly's series yet, get <u>Mystic Pieces</u> here. You can also save a buck by getting the boxed set.

GET A FREE NOVELLA!

If you sign up for my newsletter at www.adabell.com, you will receive *Mystic Treasure*, the story of what happened on that momentous day. Just a little gift from me to you.

After a busy winter of murder-solving, Aly can't wait to relax with some family fun at the Shady Grove Annual Treasure Hunt. For twenty-five years, town residents have searched futilely for a chest containing the deed to an abandoned mansion on the edge of town. At this point, Aly's pretty sure the treasure is a myth, but she's always up for Shady Grove shenanigans.

When the Treasure Hunt gets underway, a suspicious new resident throws everything into question. Someone's got a hidden motive for participating, and the town may be in danger. Can Aly solve the mystery to save the day?

MYSTIC TREASURE
A SHADY GROVE NOVELLA
ADA BELL

MYSTIC TREASURE PREVIEW

Today was the perfect day to win a fortune. I wasn't the only one who thought so: The Shady Grove Town Square hummed with excitement. Fluffy white cumulus clouds peppered the sky. Between the slight breeze and the mercury topping out at seventy degrees, this was the kind of gorgeous summer day that made it worth living through the humidity and thundershowers.

Half the town must have turned out to watch this event. Granted, half the town meant a few thousand people, but still. Town Square was bursting at the seams. Set near the end of Main Street, the largest park in town ran a block down to Second Street, with the other end across the street from City Hall. My three-year-old nephew and I stood under a tree, soaking it all in while we waited for my brother to join us.

Thankfully, Kyle hadn't yet seen the guy making balloon animals. On the corner nearest me, a marching band warmed up their instruments, complete with a bagpipes player. Town residents milled around, visiting the booths that had been set up to feed and entertain us. A huge banner extended across the square, welcoming everyone to the "WALTER SPARROW ANNUAL MEMORIAL TREASURE HUNT".

According to the rumor mill, Walter Sparrow was some eccentric millionaire who died about twenty-five years ago. Instead of leaving his money to a relative or a friend or a local animal shelter, he created this big annual party for everyone to try to win the big prize. No one had managed yet. My best friend Rusty suspected the entire story was a lie, and Walter just wanted to make sure we all talked about him forever after he passed.

Considering the amount of money supposedly on the line, I was surprised there weren't fortune hunters sniffing around all year, but Shady Grove wasn't like other towns. Maybe the same forces that led to unusual happenings kept outsiders away?

Or our town was so tiny that no one outside a fifty-mile radius had heard of Shady Grove or old Walter? That was more likely.

Personally, I suspected Rusty was right. The whole thing sounded like an urban legend. An excuse for a big summer party, but anyone expecting to find treasure would be sorely disappointed. Still, we'd teamed up and gotten ready for action. The practice solving clues should come in handy once Rusty finished getting his PI license.

Tugging my hand, Kyle peered up at me with his big brown eyes and heart-shaped face from beneath his adorably oversized sun hat. "What's a treasure hunt, Aunt Aly?"

I resisted smoothing an errant chestnut curl that was so like mine. "It means Rusty and I are going to follow clues to find a lost item that has been hidden somewhere in the town."

"I find it! What did Rusty lose?" Kyle asked.

I grinned at the spark of excitement in his eyes and smoothed a curl off of his forehead. My nephew had been born with the power to find lost objects, a secret we preferred to keep from the rest of the world as long as possible. Psychic powers ran in our family, but we'd recently learned that some people wanted to exploit what he could do. "Thanks, Little Man, but this game is for adults only. Besides, in a game, it's not fair to use our special abilities to win."

"Cheating?"

"Yes, that's considered cheating."

"Oh. I won't cheat." Kyle stuck out his lower lip. Then his gaze landed on one of the tables below the "WALTER SPARROW MEMORIAL TREASURE HUNT" banner. "Cookie?"

With a laugh, I let him drag me to the table, manned by my friend and the owner of the local coffee shop, Julie Capaldi. A self-described "recovering lawyer," Julie was a blue-eyed blonde who'd moved to Shady Grove a few years ago to take over her aunt's business. She'd set out cookies for sale, but also—and more importantly—iced coffee.

"Hey! Looking forward to the hunt?" she asked when we got within earshot.

"You know it," I said. "Rusty's excited to practice his PI skills. I'm here to stop him from picking the locks of every store on Main Street."

She laughed. "He's going to be a great investigator. I miss having him at the cafe, though."

Until recently, Rusty had worked as the manager at On What Grounds?. After helping me learn to use my powers and solve a murder, my new best friend discovered his true calling. I often considered myself fortunate Julie hadn't banned me from her store when he left. Where would I get my coffee?

Then again, I suspected she had a thing for my brother.

"Hey, kiddo!" she said to Kyle before offering him a cookie. "You planning to hunt treasure today?"

"Aunt Aly said I was cheating."

My face flamed. Maybe she wouldn't understand him? Three-year-olds didn't have the best enunciation, and his mouth was full of cookie. I wasn't sure how much Julie knew, either about Kyle's abilities or mine. She certainly hadn't heard it from me, but small towns didn't have many secrets.

"Cheating? That's no good." She gave me one of those 'kids say the darnedest things' grins.

In response, I gave her the most innocent look I could muster. "We're learning new words this week. Anyway, are you entering?"

"No, I can't."

"Can't?"

She shook her head and laughed. "I did it last year. You're only allowed to enter once."

"That's odd," I said. "Kevin did it last year, too. I thought he wasn't entering because he wanted to spend the day with Kyle."

"That's part of it, I'm sure. But yeah, everyone gets one chance." She shrugged. "People with money are eccentric, right? It's Walter's estate, so he gets to make the rules. I'll send all my good vibes to you and Rusty."

At the mention of my partner, I turned to scan the crowd. With the pre-hunt festivities drawing to an end, Town Square had cleared out somewhat. A lot of people still stood around, but most moved to ring the center, where the hunt would soon begin.

About fifteen feet away, I spotted my friend Tiffaneigh Pratt talking to Brad Stevens. The three of us studied science together at Maloney College. She still didn't want to admit they were dating, but the two of them looked awfully cozy. Their matching bright blue shirts with "WALTER SPARROW HUNTER" on the back told me everything I needed to know about their relationship—and my primary competition. Tiffaneigh hated to lose, and she had some flexible ideas about what constituted fair and legal gameplay.

We'd need to keep an eye on her if we wanted to win.

Mystic Treasure is ONLY available by signing up for my newsletter - visit www.adabell.com to get your copy.

ALSO BY ADA BELL

Shady Grove Psychic Mysteries

Ever since 21-year-old Aluminum Reynolds moved to Shady Grove, New York, life has been full of surprises. She never believed in psychics, until the day she got hit with a vision.

Mystic Pieces: Aly doesn't believe in psychics. Too bad she just had her first vision. Her first instinct is flat-out denial. After all, science and magic don't mix. But when a man is murdered, Aly realizes she may be able to use her strange new "gifts" to find the culprit. If she can avoid getting herself killed in the process.

The Scry's the Limit: Aly's starting to get the hang of her psychic gifts when she literally stumbles over her favorite professor's body. She's devastated and determined to get justice. But with several people benefitting from Professor Zimm's death, how will Aly find the real culprit before they find her?

Sight Seering: As a psychic who gains powers from antiques, Aly is ecstatic to be invited to an estate sale. It's only after she arrives that she discovers the estate's owner didn't die in her sleep—she was murdered.

Mystic Treasure: Aly and Rusty are excited to participate in the annual Walter Sparrow Treasure Hunt. As the event gets underway, they realize there's more to this event than meets the eye. Someone's got a hidden motive for participating, and the entire town may be in danger.

Seer Today Gone Tomorrow: Just when Aly finally identified her sister-in-law's killer, they got away—and they're not alone. To make matters worse, someone powerful has cursed the residents of Shady Grove. Aly's powers vanish. Without her psychic gifts, how will Aly find Katrina's killer and save the pet store?

The Pie in the Scry: After nearly a year, Aly's got a plan to bring Katrina's killer to justice. But before she and Kevin can implement it, she has a vision of someone murdering Tony, the bakery owner. As if that wasn't bad enough—the killer looks exactly like Aly.

Mystic Persons: Aly just completed the biggest spell she's ever attempted, with a little help. But the magic came with an unexpected side effect, and now she's got to figure out what happened to the dead man in the upstairs bath before her parents arrive for the holidays.

The Psychic's the Thing: At her roommate's urging, Aly tries out for the college play. She's surprised to be cast as understudy to the lead—but not nearly as shocked as when the star turns up dead.

Haunted Haven Mysteries

Emma thought life was weird before she found out she was a witch. Now she's got some pretty cool powers, a snarky-yet-insightful talking cat, and a fabulous mansion-turned-B&B, complete with ghost. Here is your complete guide to the *Haunted Haven* series.

<u>Unfinished Witchness:</u> Emma is thrilled to come into her legacy: not only has she inherited stacks of money and a mansion, she's got magic! Everything is coming up roses until she finds her new chef dead in the kitchen and her other employee accused of murder. If she can't find the real killer, this haunted haven might never open for business.

<u>Risky Witchness:</u> Now that Emma's bed and breakfast is bustling with activity, she decides to treat herself to some R&R at the local fancy spa. But when she finds another guest dead, Emma becomes the prime suspect. She'll need the help of his ghost to help find the real killer before they find her.

Open for Witchness: When Ben convinces Emma to investigate the mysteriously closed bar in Shady Grove, she discovers it's being guarded by an extremely unpleasant spirit. The only way to help her friend is to solve the mystery—but the trail has been cold for decades. Can she close the case and reopen the bar?

Bundles and Boxed Sets

Shady Grove Psychic Mysteries 1-3

Shady Grove Psychic Mysteries 4-6

Haunted Haven Mysteries 1-3

ABOUT THE AUTHOR

Ada Bell is an award-winning author who thought that it would be cool to use a secret identity when writing mysteries. After all, who doesn't want a secret identity? She doesn't remember where the idea for the Shady Grove mysteries started, but she freely admits that Kyle is based on a certain precious toddler in her own life. Ada loves Scooby Doo, superhero movies, STEM heroines, and cake. Mmm, cake.

Find Ada online at www.adabell.com, or get access to sneak peeks, news and more by joining her Facebook group or mailing list.